END OF EXISTENCE

A Kirkland Finn Adventure

ANDY MUNRO

Copyright

Cover design by A Munro.

First Edition @ Jan/2021

ASIN : Paperback : B08X63FJDY
ASIN : eBook : B08X4Z146L
ISBN-13 : 9798712675920

More books in the Kirkland Finn series

2020 - Finn's Quest (Book 1) - ASIN: B08RH5N1RL

Acknowledgement

This book would not have been possible without the support of my partner Christine McLoughlin who was involved from the start. Thank you, Christine, for your support and encouragement. Taking the time to read each new chapter, commenting on how the plot developed and giving me valuable guidance.

I would also like to say thanks to all my friends whose comments and feedback has given me the encouragement to continue writing more books. I appreciate all the kind words that I received for Finn's Quest, book 1 in the Kirkland Finn series. Special thanks go to Paul & Ros, Paul & Andrea, Alan & Katherine, John, Richie, Trevor, Stewy, Karl, Daz, Paul H, Mel, Pauline, Judith, Mick, Jamie and all the other DRAC lads.

Table of Contents

About the Author

I am a retired design engineer from the North East of the UK. END OF EXISTENCE is the second book I have published in the Kirkland Finn series, more will follow.

I published my first book in December 2020, FINN'S QUEST. The book introduced two main characters, Kirkland Finn, a Captain in the SAS, and FBI special agent Nico Torres. Finn's Quest tells the story of the kidnapping of Finn's sister while she is on holiday. Armed men have taken her from a remote campsite in New Mexico, killing her friends in the process. Torres informs Finn, currently deployed in Afghanistan, of the kidnapping. Finn pulls in some favours and travels to the USA. The two men work together, revealing a web of corruption which spreads across the various US intelligence agencies. Follow Finn's Quest to find his sister. From the forests of New Mexico, through the streets of El Paso, to Lubbock, Akron and onwards to Afghanistan. Can Finn find his sister in time?

I am in the process of writing a set of seven Western pocket books and plan to write a series of crime thrillers featuring FBI agent Nico Torres.

Look out for my books on Amazon. They are available in eBook, Kindle, and Paperback format. I hope you like this book and will consider my other publications.

Contact via twitter using @KirklandFinn

Andy

Prologue

Ilya took the ice cream from his mother. Now in his eighth year he yearned for the day when she would allow him to go out and play by himself. He tasted the vanilla flavouring and continued to wait patiently at the roadside for her to finish paying.

From the pavement he looked along the row of grey concrete tower blocks that stretched out in front of him towards the research facility building. He thought of his father. Like most of the residents of Yacheyka, his father went there every day to work, leaving the empty streets to married women and children.

The summer sun generated a heat haze that rose above the research facility. He liked the summer, a time away from school.

He flinched when his mother dropped her change on the floor. He looked back to see her staring at the research facility and did the same. The heat haze now a grey mist approached, pushed along by the light breeze.

There was a scream and a car horn sounded. A bus ran off the road and hit a wall. A car drove past at high speed, out of control, the driver slumped at the wheel. He watched as it began swerving, mounted the curb and ran into a tree. People began falling, their faces blackened and frozen in pain as the mist consumed them.

Trees and bushes lost their leaves, shrivelling and falling like black snow. Birds began falling from the sky with their wings outstretched. Grass died and blew away leaving blackened patches of soil.

Ilya froze as the vapor swept over him. He dropped the ice cream as the first particles entered his lungs. The tiny germ raced into his bloodstream, tearing the young life from him in a moment. His blackened corpse fell to the pavement next to his mother.

Chapter 1
Hereford, UK

Kirkland Finn put his empty pint glass down on the table and looked around the bar. The Rose and Crown pub in Hereford town centre was quiet for a Saturday afternoon. Only the bartender and Jim were there to keep him company. The only noise was from the television on the wall. The presenter was announcing that the midday premiership game was about to start.

Jim, the old soldier, still wearing his army greatcoat and beret, was asleep in his usual chair with a flat half empty pint of bitter in front of him. His devoted dog Sally, a Jack Russell, also in her sunset years, sat patiently next to his legs.

Finn's attention turned to the bartender, a middle-aged woman of ample proportions, their eyes met and she smiled. He walked to the bar and purchased another pint of real ale. As always, Finn bought an extra one for Jim. The bartender put the money on the side of the till and promised to give it to him later. He considered asking her if there was anything that she would consider giving him later. He cast the thought aside when he noticed her wedding ring.

As he returned to his seat he picked up a discarded newspaper and began reading the latest junk. He flicked through the pages reading stories about lying politicians, unruly pop stars, overpaid footballers moaning and price rises. He returned to page three as that held something of interest.

He was just starting to enjoy the peace and quiet when

3

a group of five young men entered shouting and talking loudly to each other. At the bar they began barking out orders to the bartender, pints of lager and shots.

Finn put his paper down and studied the men. It didn't take him long to identify them as football fans on a Saturday away game day out, visiting the town to see their team play in the lower divisions of the football league. A day on the drink with a bit of football in the middle to help sober them up. The casual clothes, north east accents and the repeated sexist comments to the bartender gave it away.

One of the men shouted, "Pool!"

He watched as they moved towards the rear of the bar where the pool table, and old Jim, were located. Of the five individuals he could see there was a leader, the alpha male, the one who was constantly shooting his mouth off, bossing the others about. From the foot soldiers, Finn could see that only one, possibly two, would put up a fight.

Bored with watching their antics Finn continued drinking his pint and reading the paper. He heard one of the men announce, "Look at this silly old sod, he thinks he's still at war."

He looked up to see one of the foot soldiers standing over Jim. The old soldier woke, bleary eyed, and stared at the young man unsure of what was happening. Another foot soldier snatched the beret from Jim. He put the beret on his own head and began jumping around like the village idiot. In the process he knocked over the old man's pint and stepped on the dog's paw. The dog gave out a whelp and hid under the table. The other men all laughed loudly, proud of the two idiots' performance, bullying an old man and hurting his dog.

Finn's eyes narrowed as the idiots started throwing the beret around to each other, trying it on in between each throw. Eventually it landed on the floor. One of the idiots kicked it into the main bar and shouted, "Goal!"

Finn put down his paper and drank off his pint. History had told him that it was unlikely he would get the chance later. He climbed from the comfort of his chair, moved to the rear of the bar and approached the men. In a calming tone he said, "Come on guys show some respect."

The comment passed over the void between the alpha male's ears. Unable to form an intellectual response he grunted, "What's it got to do with you? Well dickhead? You want your head kicking in, or what?"

"I'll go for what."

The comment caught Alpha off guard, "Eh?"

Finn continued, "Look moron, that guy has more courage in his ball sack than you five idiots have put together. Now apologise, buy him a pint and fuck off somewhere else."

The bartender started picking the glasses off the bar, putting them behind her out of the way.

The five football fans gathered and studied the man standing in front of them. Short cropped hair, tanned face, brown leather jacket, white t-shirt, jeans and adidas trainers. To them he looked like another middle-aged bloke getting some peace and quiet away from the wife and kids. Another worker getting his weekly dose of beer and television football.

"Been on the sun bed mate?" Alpha quipped, then added, "You'd better fuck off before you get hurt."

Finn considered the comment and realised he was

5

referring to the tan he'd acquired fighting terrorists in Afghanistan. He was supposed to be on leave, instead he was home and confronted by a different type of terrorism. He reached down, picked up the beret, dusted it off and handed it to the old man. The five hooligans moved closer and Finn realised he was trapped between the men, old Jim, and the pool table. He quickly pushed past the men into the main bar area, making space for himself.

"That's right, run off to mummy," one of the foot soldiers shouted.

Having created a modest area for himself to work in, Finn turned and faced the men. Behind him the doorway, to his left the bar and on his right a row of seats. Finn took up a defensive stance and looked at the men, as he had guessed earlier, two had petrified looks on their faces. He summarised the situation in his head, mapping out how to narrow the odds in his favour.

Alpha picked up Jim's broken glass and growled, "Come on! Let's have it."

He moved towards Finn with the glass in his right hand. As he lunged forward Finn batted his hand away using his left arm then hit Alpha full in the face with his right fist. Alpha's nose burst open and blood began pouring down onto his lips and chin. After stumbling, Alpha lunged forward again, urged on by his mindless friends with the glass still drawn.

Finn dodged to his right and knocked over a table, the jagged glass missed his face by an inch. Alpha lunged again, Finn picked up a chair, held it by the backrest and used the legs as a shield. The glass shattered into small pieces and fell from the hooligan's hand.

Alpha, now unarmed, looked to his men for support, three against one were his usual odds. Two joined him and all three rushed at the SAS soldier. Their usual battle tactics. Overpower a victim, get them on the floor and kick the hell out of them. A simple strategy that had proved fruitful in the past, but not on guys like Finn. During his military career he had regularly fought three or more foes, most were dead.

Predicting the assault, Finn banged the wooden chair on the floor, breaking it into pieces and picked up a leg. Now armed he battered Alpha across the head knocking him out. The force of the club threw his body sideways, hitting his head on the bar and knocking his front teeth out. As the next foot soldier advanced Finn used the wooden leg as a ram into the man's stomach, raised it and caught him under the chin. His body flew backwards onto the carpet. The last foot soldier came forward for his punishment. Finn kicked him in the groin with the precision of a professional footballer. The hooligan bent forward grabbing feverishly at his injured tackle. Finn finished him off with a blow to the head with the wooden batten.

It was over as quickly as it started.

Finn looked down at the three battered and bleeding men laid out in front of him. The other two had already left by the rear door.

Jim saluted him and raised his pint in a gesture of solidarity. The dog came out from under the table wagging its tail. Finn returned the salute then moved over to the bartender who had a grin on her face. He rummaged in his jean pocket, pulled out a ten-pound note, threw it on the bar and said, "Sorry about the chair."

"Never mind that! You should get going before the law turns up."

"Good point."

Finn left the bar via the front door, walked down the street and into the Turks Head.

❖ ❖ ❖ ❖

Adams walked into the Turks Head and headed to the bar, "I thought I might find you here."

Through blurry eyes Finn looked up from the bar to see Adams, his CO, standing next to him with two military police officers.

"How many have you had?"

"Not enough!" Finn slurred.

"You're lucky that you're not locked up. Those guys you beat up are in hospital, one has a fractured skull. I had to convince the police to drop it and let me arrest you."

"You and whose army," Finn boasted as he tried to get off the bar stool. Adams grabbed his arm to stop his fall.

"Come on…let's get you back to base, they've got a new job for you."

The two MP's grabbed Finn under the armpits and dragged him outside to the jeep. They threw him in through the rear door and he laid out on the metal flatbed mumbling something to himself. Adams climbed in the rear and sat on the wheel arch with the prone soldier at his feet.

The British Army jeep headed out of town towards RAF Credenhill on the A438, joining the A480 onwards to the camp gates. The journey to Sterling Lines, the designated name of the garrison of the 22nd SAS based at Credenhill, took twelve minutes. During the drive Finn managed to drag himself up from the floor then was promptly sick over the rear door and collapsed again.

Adams considered the toll that the previous six months in Afghanistan had taken on his second in command. Add to that the stress of dealing with the kidnapping of his sister and he could understand why Finn needed to let off steam.

"I don't want the men seeing him like this, take him to the cells and get him sobered up. When he's fit enough, bring him to my office."

Chapter 2
RAF Credenhill

Finn woke with a headache. He rose from the wooden bench and looked around the holding cell, the memories of the day before slowly returning. He aggressively rubbed his face and head to supress the headache, then climbed from the bench and banged on the steel door, "Come on guys let me out!"

After a few moments he heard a key in the lock and stepped back. The door swung open and he was greeted by a young MP with a grin like a cat, "Morning Captain, how do you feel today? The guys are wondering if you fancied ordering room service, we've got a Full English on the menu."

He focused his eyes on the young soldier and rubbed his head again, "I've got a steam train running through my head son, so less of the wise cracks. How did I end up here?"

"You were propping up the bar in the Turks Head, luckily for you the bartender called here before the local police found you. Adams has sorted everything out with the locals. If you're up and about you should get over to his office straight away. I'll take you in my jeep."

"I need to clean myself up first and get into uniform, can you stop by my place on the way? Also, grab me a bacon butty."

"No problem, but don't forget next time you're abroad to pick up a bottle of malt at the duty free for me and the lads."

Finn smiled and the two men proceeded outside. After a quick shower and change of clothes they completed the short journey to the admin building and Adam's office.

The MP knocked quickly, opened the door, and announced, "Captain Finn sir."

"Ah, good, get your arse in here Finn we've a job for you," Adams announced.

Finn walked in asking, "We?"

The MP shut the door behind him and that's when he noticed a man on his left looking out of the window. Finn noted the Saville Row suit, highly polished shoes, and a distinct smell of bullshit.

Adams recognised the look on Finn's face, "Take a seat Captain."

Finn sat down then looked at the mystery man and quipped, "Who's the suit?"

"This gentleman is from MI6. He needs to talk to you urgently about a matter of national security."

Finn stared as the middle-aged man turned to face him. His neat black hair tinged with grey matching the lines on his pinstripe suit. The man showed no emotion on his face, despite Finn's dismissive comment, instead taking out a silver cigarette case from his inside pocket. After lighting a cigarette, he sat on the windowsill and took a long drag. He continued to stare at Finn, blew the smoke towards the floor and announced, "Your reputation follows you

Captain Finn. I've read all about your recent adventures in the US and Afghanistan. Your friend Colby speaks very highly of you."

"That sounds great but seeing as you know my name, how about telling me yours?"

"My name is not important at this stage but let's just say that my job is to ensure that foreign organisations don't interfere with our country's interests."

Finn shook his head in disbelief, "The man with no name? Typical! So why am I here?"

"Have you ever heard of a place called Yacheyka?"

"No!" Finn replied in a sarcastic tone. "Should I have?"

"Yacheyka is a town in the north of Russia, about eight hundred miles from Moscow, close to Finland. It's no surprise that you haven't heard of it as it doesn't exist on any published maps, but it's there. The Russians established it just after the second world war. At that time Russia was hellbent on setting up lots of new weapons manufacturing and research facilities in remote locations, hard to access and easy to hide. They were competing with the Americans to create improved weapons that would give them an edge in the arms race. Each new research facility was set up from scratch and had a town built around it for the workers and their families. They built the new towns in isolated places, cut off from the outside world. Locations that provided maximum security and deniability. The state provided everything to keep the workers happy, homes, shops, schools, bars, parks, recreation facilities. One such place is Yacheyka."

"And why are you telling me this?"

The man walked over to Adam's desk, picking up a folder. He took out a piece of paper and handed it to Finn, "That is an aerial photograph of Yacheyka taken in nineteen fifty-seven. You can see the facility and the town. Looks just like a regular town, doesn't it?" He reached into the file and took out a second picture, "This one was taken in nineteen sixty-four."

Finn took the second image, holding an image in each hand, he compared them. The first showed a town with a large circular building at one end. The roads leading out from the building led to rows of tower blocks. He picked out football fields and other recreational areas scattered on the outer edges and one single road leading away from the town across a barren landscape. He followed the road and spotted a few miles from the town a large military guard post. The second image showed the same scene except the circular building now had a hole in the roof. Sweeping out from the damaged building up to a radius of ten miles there was a blackened scar on the land. The structures were still there, tower blocks and other buildings but the trees, bushes and grass now black, stripped of all life. On the roads and pavements, he noticed bodies and crashed cars. He continued to look at the images. After a short period of time he asked, "So what happened? An explosion of some kind?"

"There was an explosion, you're right, but that was just the trigger. Yacheyka was a biological weapons research facility, set up by the Russians to create, investigate and test new strains of germ warfare. What you can see in the second image is the result of one of these new biological weapons escaping. We don't know the full details of what happened. It appears there was an accident of some kind, causing an explosion, which triggered the release of a biological weapon into the atmosphere. The pathogen was deadly, every living organism that met the biological strain died, instantly. Generally, when scientists are developing these things they work on tiny samples. Therefore, we assume that a small amount escaped, but regardless it still did a hell of a lot of damage. Just imagine what a larger sample could do. The incident scared the crap out of the Russians. They immediately put in a fifty-mile exclusion zone around the town and shut down their other biological weapons facilities. They guard the exclusion zone twenty-four hours a day from the military garrison on the fifty-mile perimeter. Since the accident, in sixty-four, no one has ever entered the exclusion zone. There's an unwritten agreement between Russia and NATO that no one goes there. In the early eighties the Russian's positioned a geosynchronous satellite over the place to monitor it day and night. NASA has access to the satellite feed and we've been watching ever since. That's until yesterday when the satellite feed suddenly stopped."

"A technical fault?" Finn suggested.

"Possible, but unlikely. NASA have confirmed the satellite is still there and transmitting, however it appears a signal from within the exclusion zone is jamming it. The Russians have not responded to our requests to confirm the situation on the ground. Instead, we've started picking up a lot of radio traffic from the garrison that suggested something was happening on the ground. The Russians have also started transmitting coded messages to their agents across Europe. Unfortunately, they're using a new code system. We're working on cracking it so we can read the messages but that type of work takes time. Something we don't have."

"You didn't come all this way to give me a tourist information briefing on holiday travel in Russia. The fact I'm here suggests you want me to do something that you can deny later."

The man smirked, "Colby said you're the best covert operative that he's worked with outside of the US and that's what we need. Do you fancy a trip to Russia?"

The question intrigued Finn, "Go on."

"We need you to go to Yacheyka and find out what has happened since the satellite link failed. We need you to identify where the jamming signal is originating from and who's behind it. Yacheyka is a place frozen in time. We're seriously concerned why it has suddenly become active. All the data related to this biological weapon is still on site, the samples, formula, test results, everything. We don't want it getting into the wrong hands."

The man opened the file and placed a map of the area on Adam's desk and began pointing out details while he spoke. "This is Yacheyka. You'll travel by light aircraft to an airstrip on the Finnish side of the Russian border. There you'll meet with one of our contacts, Petrikov, a Russian.

He'll get you over the border and lead you to the edge of the exclusion zone. It's going to be a hard slog. You'll be mostly on foot apart from a few miles by four-by-four and a boat. Once you arrive at the fifty-mile limit you're on your own, Petrikov will wait for you. If you're not back within forty-eight hours we'll assume you've failed and we'll have to come up with a plan B."

"Forgive me for asking but if the Russians have not let anyone in there for over fifty years does it not suggest that whatever killed those people is still there?"

"A good point Finn. Our scientists have done a risk assessment and think the danger from the original germ release may have passed. In the last few years signs of some of the vegetation returning have shown up on the satellite images, they even spotted a group of wolves roaming within the exclusion zone. What worries us is the fact that it won't have gone unnoticed by others that the place is slowly returning to normality. It appears that the Russians are still too scared to go in there, intelligence suggests that someone else has."

"So, let me get this straight, I've got to trust a risk assessment by white coated men. If they prove to be correct and the deadly biological weapon doesn't kill me it's possible that I'll get torn to pieces by a pack of dogs." Finn looked to Adams and added, "Can you just drop me off at the Turks Head instead?"

Adams replied sarcastically, "You've worn out your welcome in the town Finn, you'll be safer off site. Besides it sounds like the sort of adventure you like, I'm sure you'll do just fine."

"Is that your motivational speech?"

The MI6 man interrupted, "I forgot to say, you go tonight. We've made all the arrangements. One of my agents is waiting in the Adjutant's office with some gear that you'll need. I'll travel with you to Finland. We can talk more about the mission on the way."

Finn climbed from the chair and before he arrived at the door turned back to announce, "In that case, I need to get packed."

∴ ∴ ∴ ∴

Finn and the MI6 agent took off by helicopter from the sports field at Credenhill. At a small municipal airport near Darlington in the north east of England they transferred to a light aircraft. The small four-seater aircraft flew to Stockholm, refuelled, and continued onwards to a secluded airstrip in Finland, near the Russian border.

On the trip the two men talked.

"So how real is the threat from this weapon?" Finn enquired.

"From the documents I've seen and data handed over by our agents, it's the deadliest behind a full-on nuclear war. You looked at the image. Those bodies in the street didn't have time to react. If someone replicated and mass produced it, they could wipe out whole nations. It's not the

sort of thing we want getting into the hands of a terrorist…
or fanatic."

"So why did the spread stop there? Surely it could have
spread much further."

"All we can surmise is the combination of
environmental conditions and size of dose. No significant
winds reported on the day in question, a typical summer's
day, we can only assume a small dose escaped."

"So why leave it until now to send someone in there?
Why did the Russians not just blow the place up, or send
people in using biohazard suits?"

"The Russians were too scared of contamination getting
out. A bomb could've spread the pathogen out into the
atmosphere. And as for sending people in there…We did!"
The MI6 man paused and looked out of the aircraft window
as if considering his next words carefully. After several
minutes of silence, he turned to Finn, caution written on
his face, "I'll be straight with you Finn, that's the least you
deserve. In the late sixties we sent in a small military
group. Their goal was simple, collect tissue samples from
the victims and various plants. Once we had those, we
could analyse the cause and maybe come up with an
antidote."

"And?"

"The last transmission came when they moved into the
exclusion zone. We never heard from them again."

"So, you decided it was too dangerous?"

"No, two more missions failed, the last made up of joint
US and UK operatives. We agreed with NATO to give up

once the satellite went live. It would be good if you could confirm what happened to those guys while you're there."

"You guys are unbelievable! You dream up these wild missions and send blokes to their death without a second thought. Now I suppose it's my turn. I'm next on your bloody suicide list."

"I hear what you're saying Finn. I only became aware of this situation a few years ago myself and it was only when the satellite went off line that alarm bells rang. Once the specialists suggested that the area may be safe to enter, I proposed a one-man mission to investigate, risking one life…unlike before. After reviewing available personnel, you came out on top of the list."

"Now you tell me…when we're minutes from landing. Is there any more important information that you're keeping from me?"

"No…you know what I know. Just get in there and see what you can find, we need intel."

"Tell me about the Russian I'm meeting."

"Petrikov? He's been on our books for years. He moves a lot between Finland and Russia and from what I know he's lived near the exclusion zone. Overall, my experience of working with him is sound. When you arrive at the airstrip you've got a short hike to the coordinates that have been sent to your iBOW device."

Finn took out the small handheld device from his cargo pant pocket and switched it on. He opened the GPS application, confirmed the stored location then began checking the other app and settings.

Mac added, "That's the latest military grade GPS and communication device. Apart from the route planning software you can use it for a lot of different tasks like taking photos, messaging and to store information. It also acts as a tracker so we can see where you are, it's your lifeline…so don't lose it."

"Does it play music?"

"Petrikov will meet you at zero four hundred hours… don't be late!"

Finn put away the iBOW and asked, "Can I trust this guy with my life?"

"If I was going in there, he's the one person I'd want with me."

Finn laughed out loudly, "You suit guys always say that crap when you know it won't happen. Spare me the bullshit you wouldn't go anywhere near the place if you thought you could be in danger."

"I'm here now…and I don't always wear a suit. I'm just like you Finn, we may have followed different careers but I can assure you I've seen my fair share of danger. If this thing goes pear-shaped, I'll do everything I can to get you home…that's a promise."

Finn raised his eyebrows dismissively, "A promise?"

The two men stared at each other for a moment.

Finn broke the silence, "To clarify, my mission is, go into this city, find evidence of the biological weapon, take some tissue samples and find out what happened to guys you sent out there on a suicide mission."

"More or less."

20

Chapter 3
Finland

The light plane touched down at a secluded airstrip sheltered on all sides by trees at 01:35. The pilot kept the engine running. Finn grabbed his gear, climbed out, shut the door and shouted out over the noise of the propellor, "So tell me your name. If you're going to send me to my death it would be good to know who to blame."

The MI6 man smiled and shouted, "Just call me Mac."

Finn slammed the door and watched as the plane turned around and took off into the night. He ran to the tree line and took out the iBOW device. Once online it began to display the six-point three-mile route to the meeting point. With his backpack secure he set off at a moderate pace closing the distance down within two hours.

He arrived at a disused logging cabin and checked the display on the iBOW to confirm he was in the right place. His watch displayed 03:47 and he returned to the tree line to wait. Instinctively he knew the Russian was already there, somewhere, in the woods, watching him, checking him over, waiting…just like he was.

As the time approached 04:00 he proceeded to the cabin, checked through the window for signs of life and slowly opened the door. Inside, a small oil lamp was burning, shedding dim light around the room. A table and chairs, cooking stove, camp bed and wood burner provided scant furnishings. n put his pack down and walked over to the wood burner, gently placing his hands on the warm metal casing. The dimly glowing embers inside providing evidence that workers used the cabin earlier in the day. He picked up a couple of logs from a nearby basket and chucked them inside. Within minutes flames began to appear in the glass.

04:12. Finn heard a noise from outside and took up position alongside the door. He took out his silenced pistol and held it ready. The door handle turned and the door slowly opened. As the man began to enter Finn drew the pistol out from behind the door and placed the barrel on the man's neck.

The man froze, "Is that how you greet all your guests?"

"Name?" Finn demanded.

"Really? How many other men do you think are walking around here in the middle of the night?"

"Name!" Finn pushed the barrel harder.

"Petrikov."

Finn slowly removed the pistol, "Come in."

The man walked into the room, Finn shut the door, "Turn around so I can see you." The man complied.

Finn studied his appearance. Mid to late thirties, large, over six foot tall and easily 200lbs. Short brown hair, shaved at the sides, dressed like a hiker with a rucksack, cargo pants, heavy jacket, and boots. In his belt he had a large hunting knife with a serrated edge.

"It's been a hike for me to get here. Can I at least sit down now?" Petrikov asked.

Finn gestured towards the table then put away his pistol, "Sorry about that it's an old habit."

"The sort of habit that will guarantee a longer life my friend." Petrikov sat down and unzipped his backpack pulling out a bottle, "Vodka?"

"Definitely!" Finn grabbed two dusty glasses from a shelf, quickly wiped them with his fingers then placed them down in front of the Russian. Petrikov poured out two large measures and raised his glass, Finn followed suit. They banged the glasses and Finn watched while the Russian drank his glass in one. Considering it safe to proceed Finn did the same.

After a few more glasses Finn asked, "So how do we get from here to the exclusion zone?"

"First, we'll hike into Russia. I've got a jeep ready on the other side of the border. We'll drive to the coast where I've arranged a meeting with a local sailor. We need to get to the far side of the White Sea to a point further up the Russian coastline. To do that we'll use a small fishing boat which will blend in with the other sea traffic. Once we get to the drop off point there's another hike across land to the exclusion zone. That's where we'll part ways my English friend."

"How long will it take?"

"A full day."

"Terrain?"

"The terrain is heavy going. Barren land, forests, marshland, peat bogs, covered with random ponds and small lakes."

"What about the exclusion zone? How close have you been?"

"I don't know of anyone who has gone in and survived. The locals call the place 'Gorod Mertvykh', or in English, 'City of the Dead'. Over the years there have been many stories about locals seeking fame and fortune venturing inside there. One thing we do know is they returned. Maybe Yacheyka killed them or maybe the Russian army did. Who knows?"

"What about recent activity, any rumours?" Finn enquired.

"In the last week military presence has increased. I think the military suspects that someone has tried once again to go in but they've not got the courage to go inside and check. Remember, whatever killed all the people in the sixties was deadly. If the biological substance is still active and someone goes in, you're risking contamination and the pathogen getting outside. There's lots of land in Russia, ignoring a section, especially wasteland like that, is easily done."

Finn finished his Vodka, stood up and collected his pack, "We should get a move on then."

Petrikov did the same, turned off the oil lamp and they left the cabin. The journey began with a moderate hike along a forest road until Petrikov turned into the forest and began walking between the trees. The Russian walked five to ten feet ahead of Finn, checking his footing and the surrounding areas as he walked. After an hour they came to an opening. Petrikov stopped and knelt at the tree line,

Finn caught up and did the same. The sun began to rise, revealing the open barren land ahead. Twenty feet in front of the treeline there was a high wire fence. On the other side, a large ditch followed by another high fence. Beyond, a dirt track ran parallel with the fence. Despite the remoteness of the location the track showed signs of regular use.

Petrikov whispered, "The border. We'll cross into Russia here. There are no guard huts for miles on either side but regular patrols drive the dirt road. At this time of day, we should be able to get through easy enough, but be careful. They have planted mines randomly in the area between the fences. They also use portable listening devices that they move around. Walk only where I walk and do exactly what I do.

Finn nodded in acceptance.

Petrikov proceeded out into the open ground and up to the fence. Finn could see that someone had cut the fence in the past with a replacement section put in place to fool the guards. Petrikov detached the wire mesh and climbed inside, holding it open for Finn. Once inside Petrikov bent back the wire tabs and sealed the fence.

He whispered, "If animals get into the neutral zone in the middle, they'll set off the mines warning the guards that there's an opening in the fence. All along the border there are openings like these used by locals to smuggle goods backwards and forwards. The black economy of the wilderness."

Without warning the Russian scrambled down the edge of the ditch and lifted a plank with grass on one side. He laid it across the ditch and rushed over to the other side. Finn did the same. Petrikov hid the plank, climbed up towards the wire fence, opened a pre-made panel and both men ventured to the other side. After sealing the fence Petrikov checked up and down the dirt track then ran over to the safety of the tree line beyond, with Finn close behind.

"Welcome to Russia my friend," Petrikov announced.

"Doesn't look that much different to Finland," Finn quipped.

Petrikov smiled, "That's the easy part over, now our journey gets much harder, follow me."

Finn logged the coordinates of his current position into the iBOW, ensuring he could find his way back to Finland if something happened to Petrikov. They hiked eight miles through the forest, eventually arriving at a small village. Petrikov opened the garage door on an abandoned building and rushed inside. After spending a few minutes trying to get the engine started he drove out in an old Lada Niva four by four.

Finn climbed in the passenger seat, "A classic!"

"Not in these parts my friend. It's exactly what we need to blend in with the locals."

Petrikov floored the accelerator and they began the five-hour drive to the coast.

Arriving on the outskirts of the town of Kem, Petrikov stopped the jeep on a grass verge and turned to Finn,

"We're now heading into the town. Let me do all the talking. The people here are Karelian, more Finnish than Russian I suppose, but that fact makes their allegiances sit somewhere between the two nations. Put your hat on and cover your face with a scarf. Once we're on the fishing boat make sure you stay below deck. The seas around here have regular navy patrols and there's a big submarine base at Severodvinsk that we must sail past."

"No problem," Finn confirmed.

Petrikov struggled with the gears on the old four by four, an example of Russian cold war engineering, and drove into the historic town. Finn noticed the old-style Russian buildings and ramshackle homes. Petrikov parked the Lada in the car park of a fish processing factory alongside many other similar vehicles. The two men continued by foot, taking the backstreets of the town until they arrived at the fish quay. Finn hid in a doorway while Petrikov spoke to a man dressed as a sailor. He watched as the Russian handed over an envelope which the sailor readily accepted. With the deal completed the two men shook hands and Petrikov waved for Finn to join him.

The sailor led them to a fishing boat and gestured for them to get on board. Once inside the wheelhouse he led them down a staircase to a small crew cabin and galley. He spoke in Russian to Petrikov, pointing towards the cooker and bunks before disappearing up the stairs.

From below Finn could hear the sailor shouting to another person. He turned to Petrikov and asked, "Can we trust him? Who's that he's speaking to?"

"Yes, we can trust him. He has his son with him. They'll stay in the wheelhouse during the journey, plus, he only gets the other half of the money when we arrive. It'll be at least another ten hours at sea until we arrive, get some sleep."

"What happens if he decides to just kill us both and just take the money from your pack?"

"Unlikely, he's my uncle, now sleep."

Petrikov threw his pack on the bench alongside the small table and climbed onto a top bunk. Finn laid on the lower bunk and quickly fell asleep, his first in over twenty-four hours.

Chapter 4
Russia

The journey across the White Sea was mostly uneventful. Finn woke after six hours and looked at his watch, *19:13.* He felt the throbbing of the engine and the gentle rocking motion of the boat. Mixed with the sound of Petrikov snoring it seemed to create a pleasant rhythm. After a few moments getting his head together he climbed from his bunk and went to the galley. His first instinct was to find or make some coffee. Finding a warm pot of stew on the cooker top he decided to forget the coffee and have that instead. He grabbed a ladle from a hook above the cooker and filled a bowl. He sat down at the small table and began eating, filling his belly with the warm liquid full of fish, carrot, and potatoes. He tore some bread from the dry loaf on the table and mopped up the last of the liquid from the bowl.

"You seem to like Russian food my friend," Petrikov said, having woken when Finn started moving around in the galley.

"Very nice, what's it called?"

"Ukha! Fisherman's stew, very popular in this area."

"Do you want one? I'm getting a refill."

"Yes, but make sure you leave enough for the Captain and his son, we need to keep them happy."

The two men ate and finished off the last of the bread. Petrikov took two bowls to the wheel house while Finn made a fresh pot of coffee. On Petrikov's return Finn handed him a cup and asked, "How far to go?"

"Another four hours or so the Captain is currently trying to avoid the navy patrol boats. The northern fleet is based in this area so it's heavily guarded. But sometimes I think it's easier to get past many guards than just one. Correct?"

"You mean because the group becomes complacent?"

"Something like that. Anyway, let's discuss what we'll do next. Once we cross the sea the boat will take us up a small river inlet. We'll travel inland for a few miles until we reach a small fishing village. It's mostly abandoned now but we need to be cautious. We are getting close to the exclusion zone and regular boats patrol the rivers that cross the area. Once we are on solid ground we'll hike across country. You should arrive at the edge of the zone around dawn tomorrow."

"What's the terrain like?" Finn asked.

"Similar to what you found in Finland. A mixture of small wooded areas, barren lands with little vegetation, marsh land and peat bogs. It'll be heavy going my friend but I'm sure that you're used to those conditions."

Finn studied the Russian, intrigued as to why he would help him, "Why are you doing this?"

"Simple my friend, money! Is that not always the reason?"

"But to let a foreigner break into your homeland seems strange to me."

Petrikov laughed then leaned forward with a glint in his eye, "You don't think like a Russian. The state may control everything but it's human nature to have free will. I like to think that inside every communist there's a capitalist waiting to escape. You also think of Russia as one land of one hundred and fifty million people that are all the same. In fact, it's made up of many different tribes with different dialects and traditions. We Karelian don't think like the table bangers in the Kremlin. We've more important things to worry about like finding food and surviving the harsh winter months."

Finn agreed, "You make a good point."

Petrikov returned to the top bunk and began reading an old magazine left by the sailors. Finn unpacked his rucksack onto his bed and began checking his gear. He cleaned his pistol, made sure the magazines were full then placed the items next to his hunting knife on the bed. He connected the iBOW to a power outlet to charge the battery and got the night vision goggles ready to charge next. He took out a few spare items of clothing and at the bottom of the rucksack he found the small metal case that Mac had given him. He flipped the clasp which opened to reveal several empty glass containers, the sample jars. He quickly locked the case, wrapped it with some clothes and replaced it at the bottom of the rucksack.

"So why are you doing this?" Petrikov asked.

Finn thought about his response then said dryly, "It's my job. I've been in the army my whole working life. I guess I must be good at it because they seem to keep promoting me, sending me on suicide missions and giving me medals."

Finn waited in silence for a response, then heard Petrikov snoring. He smiled to himself then repacked his gear, leaving the electrical items to charge. Curiosity got the better of him and he slowly moved up the stairs to the wheelhouse. The old sailor at the wheel noticed him on the stairs and waved for him to return. Finn quickly looked left out of the window and observed the shape of a navy vessel passing by with a searchlight moving along the boat. He jumped down into the crew cabin and froze. After several moments the fisherman's son appeared and spoke in broken English, "You can come up now, the ship has gone."

Finn followed him up to the wheelhouse. He scanned the area around him through the windows, seeing land on his right and the open sea on his left. The old sailor handed him a half empty bottle of vodka. Finn unscrewed the cap, took a large gulp then handed it back. The sailor did the same, smiled a toothless grin, said something in Russian and gave it back.

Finn held on to the bottle, shrugged his shoulders and the son translated, "He said 'Take it with you, it'll be cold tonight."

Finn thanked the man, took the bottle downstairs, and stashed it in his rucksack. Petrikov snored while Finn laid on his bunk. He listened to the boat and rested his eyes.

❖ ❖ ❖ ❖

The fisherman's son woke them as the boat began traveling into the river inlet and said in a concerned voice, "It's not far now we must be quick."

The two men grabbed their gear and got ready. Finn stashed the night vision binoculars, now fully charged, into his rucksack and filled his jacket pockets with a hunting knife, silenced pistol, and the iBOW. The two men quickly ate more Ukha, filling their bellies for the long hike ahead. They then joined the old man and his son in the wheelhouse.

Finn opened the small door out onto the deck and surveyed the area ahead. With no electric lighting in the wilderness to disturb the scene, he marvelled at a landscape lit by the moon. The river was calm and the moonlight glinted off the water.

The sailor slowed the boat as it approached a small jetty on the left. Once the bow of the boat was level with the jetty the son gathered a rope from the deck and made the perilous jump onto the wooden boards. Finn watched as the wooden jetty swayed under the young man's weight. Without any concern the son tied the rope to a wooden post and the sailor reversed the engines, slowing the boat to a stop. As the son pulled on the rope the boat scrapped along the wood and he shouted, "Jump."

Petrikov jumped the gap, landed on the jetty, and ran to the end where it joined the river bank. Finn did the same, stopping for a moment to look back and see the young man jumping onto the boat deck. The sailor quickened the engines and turned the around, returning towards the sea.

Joining Petrikov at the end of the jetty Finn whispered, "We've made it this far at least."

Petrikov quietly laughed and said, "The easy part is over now we must be very careful. We now have Russian soldiers, wild animals, and the terrain to worry about. Watch your footing, if you get stuck in a peat bog, I may not be able to get you out. Stay behind me."

Finn checked the iBOW. *Sixty-four miles to the facility.*

The two men set off at a fast-walking pace into the night. Every few hours Petrikov would stop for a rest and they would share some vodka. As the sun began to rise, they came upon a vast expanse of low-level ground. Finn could see patches of vegetation and clumps of trees. He cautioned at the fact that there was limited cover available for travelling in daylight hours.

Petrikov stopped when he noticed a military helicopter flying at low level towards them. He ran towards some longer grass and dived for cover, Finn followed and did the same. As they laid on the ground Petrikov said, "We are now in the exclusion zone. The helicopters fly around the perimeter. Once we get further inside, we'll be clear of them."

"Wait a moment, what's this we? I thought you were staying outside?"

"I've decided to keep you company. We'll travel a little further together and see if we can find an old farm building to use as a base. I'll wait for you there."

Finn was unsure of why the plan had changed. His instincts told him to be careful. When people change plans it's normally for their own reasons. With the Russian's understanding of the terrain a benefit to him, he decided to go along with the idea, for now.

The helicopter passed overhead and flew onwards.

Finn looked the iBOW to confirm the time and remaining distance. *Forty-three miles to the facility, 07:36.*

The two men stood up and continued hiking for another few hours, constantly checking their surroundings for activity. In the distance Petrikov spotted an old, partially collapsed farm building. He pointed and said, "We'll rest there for a few hours then you can continue alone."

They pushed on until they reached the building. Petrikov pulled the wooden door open and they ventured inside. Finn identified the building as a stable for keeping animals in during winter. He looked up at the roof and noted the random missing tiles allowing sunlight in so they could navigate their way around. The pair dumped their packs and sat down.

Finn looked at the iBOW display. *Thirty-two miles to the facility, 11:21.*

Petrikov opened his pack and pulled out a loaf of bread and some sausage and placed them on a cloth on the floor, "First we eat my friend."

After eating, sharing some stories and vodka, Finn sat down, rested against a wooden post and closed his eyes.

Finn woke with a jolt as if his body was activating some internal alarm. The failing sunlight made the interior of the stable dim. He looked around for the Russian. He looked at his watch, *18:38. Shit!*

Finn moved to the doorway and looked around the area outside but found no sign of Petrikov. *Where has he gone?*

He returned to his pack and quickly put on his jacket, hat, scarf and gloves, secured the pack on his back and moved to the doorway. With his pistol drawn he walked outside and into the twilight. He stood for a moment and scanned the landscape for any signs of life, or danger. After confirming that it was safe, he checked the iBOW for the direction of travel and set off.

Chapter 5
Yacheyka

Mac was right, the ground was heavy going with patches of hard ground leading to marsh land covered in spongy moss. Each time Finn found the softer and unstable ground he had to move sideways until he found a patch of solid ground. The biggest aggravation, slowing his progress the most, was the shallow ponds and large circular lakes of water. The peat bogs presented the deadliest obstacle to navigate. He shivered at the thought of stepping on the black soggy ground and having the life sucked from him as he disappeared into the sticky mess. *Not the best way to check out.*

The night sky turned a deep black with the stars clearly visible. A light mist hung over the moist ground, providing cover whilst also reducing visibility. He wrapped his scarf around his face as protection from the chilled air.

His senses ran on maximum, checking the ground condition, checking for danger, worrying about the biological weapon, and wondering where Petrikov had disappeared to. He constantly checked the iBOW and GPS application to monitor the direction and progress. *Seventeen miles, 23:47.*

He pushed on until the GPS application indicated only twelve miles to the town. He was now close to the failsafe line. To his left he noticed a small building on stilts, a derelict hunter's cabin. Making his way there he climbed up the small ladder and crawled inside. The floor was rotten but had enough strength to support his weight. He dropped the pack and took out his night vision binoculars. Standing at the small lookout window he scanned the area between himself and the abandoned town. The electronics picked up the heat signature of a person running away from him. *Petrikov.* He adjusted the zoom to focus in on the distant buildings where he noticed another heat signature coming from within a tower block. He marked the coordinates into the GPS application and began cautiously looking across the landscape to his left and right, *Nothing.*

Finn considered what he had observed. *What's Petrikov up to? If he wanted to get rid of me, he could have done that in Finland, on the boat or even here in the exclusion zone. He needs me alive, but for what? And who is in the tower block? The abandoned site is supposed to be empty of life.*

He saved his current location to the GPS, not sure if the small hut would come in handy later and set off towards the town. Another thirty minutes passed when he noticed the soil changing to blackened and lifeless. Suddenly he stopped. His mind working overtime, he held his breath and waited. He proceeded forward a few steps at a time, his confidence growing with each new step. After covering an additional twenty yards he decided it was probably safe and began moving freely. His eye caught a glimpse of something on the ground to his left, something that did not belong. He proceeded towards the anomaly until he was within a few feet and realised immediately what it was. Dead bodies.

He edged forward and detected from the uniforms that it was a group of six British soldiers, their bodies now skeletal and decomposed. Finn removed the dog tags and checked in the breast pocket of one of the bodies taking out a photo of a woman. He flipped it over and found the words '*Mary, 1964*' written in pencil. He stashed the dog tags and the photo into one of his cargo pants' pockets. He fumbled in the packs of a couple of the dead soldiers and pulled out their ponchos. He laid them out over the bodies and secured them with loose rocks. He stood for a moment and saluted the fallen soldiers. He took a moment to add the coordinates to the GPS then returned to his task.

When he was within three miles of the town, he stopped to take out his night vision binoculars. In front of him there was no sign of movement, only the faint light from the tower block. To ensure that he was alone he scanned the full perimeter around him.

Stowing the binoculars, he continued at a slower pace and entered the first part of the town, a road with several crashed cars, vintage models now slowly rotting away with wheel rims sitting on the dusty concrete road, the rubber long since disappeared.

Moving forward he noticed a bus crashed into a wall, a car rammed into a tree, an ice cream van faded and rusty. He identified a small and large figure laid side by side on the path in front of it, a child and adult. As he moved forward, he found more skeletal bodies laid on the pathways.

He turned into the main street. At the far end he could see the research facility building. On either side of the road large residential tower blocks that had fallen into disrepair, three on each side. Blackened tree stumps equally spaced lined the road. On the ground floor of each tower block he could see a series of commercial properties, the businesses that sold goods to the residents. He checked the GPS application on the iBOW and recalled the location of the heat signature. The small screen confirmed it as being further down the road on his right.

He took out his pistol and moved over towards the front wall of the tower block on his right and carefully edged further down the road. As he proceeded, he noticed the shop windows with plastic figures wearing shredded clothes, dusty shelves with tins of food and a cafe with skeletal remains at the front of the counter.

At the far corner of tower block one he scanned around him, more bodies and crashed cars. He ran across the intersection in the road and started moving along the front of tower block two. He checked the iBOW and the GPS application confirmed his arrival at the location of the heat signature...somewhere above him. He searched for the entrance and found a doorway central to the tower block. Pushing it open he proceeded slowly towards the stairs, gun still drawn. On the staircase the dust indicated that someone had recently used them, footprints in the dust gave it away. He looked up between the stair railings and noticed a dim red light shining above him. He counted the landings. *The fifth floor.*

Finn climbed the stairs, checking each landing for danger, once satisfied, moving higher to the next level. On the edge of the fifth-floor landing, he stopped and peeked along the row of doors, finding an open one half way down on his left. The red light from inside the room illuminated the landing. Several thick cables hung down from a hole cut in the concrete ceiling, routed into the room.

He edged his way along the landing and arrived at the doorway. He peeked inside seeing a room full with a bank of computers and other electronic equipment. He discovered a man dressed all in black sitting at a desk with his back to him. Finn edged into the room stepping carefully around the cables on the floor. Another step. *Creak.*

The computer operator looked around and glared at Finn standing five yards behind him. He reached for a pistol on the desk, giving Finn the time to advance. As he grabbed for the handle Finn launched himself on top of him, knocking the gun from his hand. The two men fell from the chair onto the floor with Finn holding onto the man's back. The man used his hands to push himself up from the floor. Finn pressed down harder but was unable to gain any pressure as his boots slipped on the dusty floor. Feeling himself losing control Finn punched the man in the ribs. The blow had no effect and the man pushed Finn away and got onto his knees.

Finn chose another tactic and punched the man in the back of the head instead. The man rocked forward absorbing a blow that would have knocked out most men, then dived to his right reaching again for the gun. Finn jumped onto the man's back again and began reaching for the gun. The pair struggled on the floor, both trying to gain an advantage.

From a radio on the desk a voice spoke in a foreign language.

Finn reached for his knife with his left hand as they both fumbled with their right-hand fingers on the handle of the pistol. Finn pressed the knife into the man's side. As the blade entered his body, the man gave out a groan. Finn pushed the blade deeper until he felt the man's body become limp.

The voice on the radio began repeating the words, now sounding desperate. Finn tried to work out the language, not Russian, possibly Scandinavian. He retrieved his knife from the body, stood up, wiped the blade on the man's back and stowed it in his belt. He kicked away the pistol and turned the body over. Checking the man's pockets, he found a mobile phone and some money. The notes said 'SVERIGES RIKSBANK'. *Swedish*.

Finn stashed the items in his rucksack. The radio fell silent and he looked at the computer screens. A digital counter on the screen indicated a time of 02:37. The electronics, coupled with the cables leading to the roof, confirmed to him that this was why the satellite had stopped working. He leaned forward to rip out the cables but stopped himself, remembering that someone had called. Disabling the system would alert the others to his presence. He took several images of the electronic equipment with the iBOW, collected a code book from the desk and headed downstairs.

Outside on the path he scanned the area for activity finding the streets empty, lifeless, frozen in time...apart from a large grey wolf staring from the other side of the road. He took out his pistol and aimed at the animal. The dog grew bored, strolled down the road and into an empty building. Finn shook his head and proceeded towards the research facility at the far end of the road. As he got closer the number of skeletal bodies grew larger. White coated corpses spread out from the entrance like a morbid fan.

Behind he heard an explosion and turned to see smoke coming from a shop front further down the road in tower block one. He waited for the smoke to clear unsure what he would find. After a few minutes of inactivity, he turned back to the task at hand and continued.

Entering the research facility was like stepping back in time, nineteen fifties architecture, decoration and furniture adorned the reception area. On the dusty floor he noticed footprints confirming that someone had entered the facility before him. He took out his pistol and began moving from the reception area down a corridor with offices. The office doors left open by fleeing occupants many years ago. Among the dust and debris, the rooms contained documents, half empty coffee cups and personal items.

He proceeded further into the building until he came to a large glass room, a laboratory with the rear corner partially collapsed. Finn assumed it was the result of an explosion in a nearby building.

The inside of the laboratory also showed signs of recent activity, documents scattered on the floors and work benches. Fridge doors open with contents, glass chemical bottles, scattered on the floor. At one workbench there was a body slumped over a set of test tubes, the decaying hand still holding a beaker. To the right of the body Finn noticed a small fridge, big enough to hold no more than ten standard test tubes. The disturbed dust confirmed that someone had recently broken the lock and removed the contents. He looked at the label on the front of the fridge door. Large red letters declared *BIOLOGICHESKAYA OPASNAST*.

Creak.

The footstep on the debris behind gave the assailant away. Finn moved quickly to his right and the stock of the rifle missed his head and hit the thick glass instead, causing a crack. Finn turned, his pistol still drawn, seeing a figure all in black standing behind him. He shot his pistol twice into the body and the figure slumped to the floor. Almost instantly bullets started hitting the glass panels around him. He dived into an open office doorway and quickly looked out and noticed another black clad figure further down the corridor, towards the reception area. He watched as the figure fired the assault rifle in measured bursts ensuring that the weapon did not overheat and jam.

With his body protected by the doorway Finn shot his pistol blindly towards the shooter. There was a loud groan of pain and the shooting suddenly ceased. Finn used the opportunity to reload then looked out of the doorway to see the shooter moving away from him, carrying a small aluminium briefcase.

Finn ran after the black clad figure, shooting as he moved. The figure slipped on the dusty floor tiles in the reception, landed on its side then instantly rolling over to face him and began shooting wildly. Finn dived behind the reception desk for cover, heard the shooter scrambling around on the floor and stood, ready to shoot, only to see the figure grab the briefcase, smash through the entrance doors and run away towards the tower block.

Finn cautiously looked around for more assailants. Confident he was alone, and too tired to start chasing people, he returned to the laboratory area. First, he searched the body of the attacker. He found a phone, Swedish money, a packet of cigarettes with a lighter inside and some condoms. He stashed the phone and money and discarded the rest.

He carefully proceeded through the open laboratory doors and began photographing the inside of the room, collecting documents as he went. He left the chemical bottles on the floor thinking that if they had any value the assailant would have taken them. Returning instead to the small fridge where he noticed that it was empty. The broken lock and lack of dust inside provided enough evidence for him to confirm that the shooter had taken the contents.

He checked around the other offices and laboratories, photographing and collecting evidence as he went. Finally deciding he was wasting his time he returned to the reception area.

As he walked towards where the figure had slipped on the dusty tiles and discovered a pool of blood. Looking closer Finn picked out a separate bloody handprint where the figure had pushed itself up from the floor. Finn took some images of the print then collected some white paper from a desk. He gently pressed it onto the bloody mark and peeled it away. He looked at the paper to confirm the print had transferred successfully, smiled to himself...then thought of Torres*.

Happy with his detective work Finn waited until the blood was dry then placed the paper between the sheets of an old magazine he found on a table. He placed the evidence in his rucksack and returned outside.

In the dust and debris on the road he discovered footprints leading away from him, mixed in with fresh spots of blood. He heard an engine start and from the shadows a large quad bike appeared. Seeing Finn, the driver quickly swung the vehicle around and sped away into the darkness between two tower blocks.

Finn looked at his watch. *03:41, the sun will be up soon.*

He walked along the road retracing his steps and observed a figure emerging from the storefront where the earlier explosion had been. He continued along the path in front of the tower block until he arrived at the location. While taking out his pistol he edged towards the opening and looked inside. The business had smashed windows and the wrecked interior pointed towards an explosion. At rear of the store he discovered a vault style door hanging on its hinges and a room with safety deposit boxes, now opened and scattered on the floor. He looked above the opening and found BANKA written in large red letters. *What the Hell!*

Having had enough excitement for one night he decided it was time to get out of the town. He recalled the location of the hunter's lookout on the GPS application and set off at a moderate pace. On the way he collected scraps of biological evidence…anything to keep Mac happy.

Arriving at the hunter's lookout as the sun came up Finn decided it was time to rest. He drank some vodka and opened a ration pack. From the lookout he used his binoculars to scan the viewable area revealing no activity in the town. On maximum zoom in the far distance, he noticed a Russian military helicopter doing a regular patrol.

After resting for an hour, he set off again towards the original farm building. The journey was hard going with the additional worry of the wolf. Finn imagined the dog gathering up his friends and waiting in the bushes for him. He arrived at the farm building at 13.48 having not seen any wolves or any other animal. Pulling open the rotten door he was surprised to find the Russian fast asleep on the floor clutching a rucksack. Next to him was a half empty bottle of vodka. Finn quietly took his pistol out, moved over to the sleeping man and kicked him.

The Russian opened his bloodshot eyes. The sight of Finn with a gun made him pull his rucksack tighter towards himself.

Finn barked, "Where the fuck did you go to?"

Petrikov stood up, "Be careful my friend, I don't like having guns pointed at me. Put it away."

"Not until you tell me what the hell is going on."

"Shopping!" Petrikov opened his rucksack to reveal a stash of jewellery and gold bars, "My task was to get you here. I decided that, while I was here, I should take the opportunity to collect up some of the items that had been left behind by the unfortunate occupants."

"You mean you came here to rob the bank?"

"Why not? All the people are dead, no one is going to miss the stuff that they left behind. And now that it looks like it's safe to enter any valuables would only end up in the pocket of some corrupt state officials. I know a superior use for it, Petrikov's retirement fund."

"I don't believe it," Finn protested.

"Also, don't forget my friend that I went inside first. I knew that if you discovered my dead body in time, you'd be able to stop and maybe get away safely."

Finn shook his head in disbelief then put his gun away, "Pass the vodka, I think I need a drink."

❖ ❖ ❖ ❖

The two men returned the same way, taking the chance to rest on the fishing boat before arriving at the town of Kem. Petrikov collected the Lada from the fish factory car park and drove towards the border. After dumping the vehicle, the two men crossed the border and Petrikov guided Finn to the logging cabin.

"This is where we say goodbye my friend," Petrikov announced. "I'm off to a Caribbean island to enjoy the rest of my life. Use your communication device to contact Mac and he'll send a plane to collect you. Stay safe my good friend, maybe our paths will cross again in the future. Petrikov put his hand into his rucksack, Finn went for his pistol. Petrikov laughed, then handed Finn a bottle, "You can finish the vodka while you're waiting." Within seconds the Russian was gone.

*Finn's Quest

Chapter 6
Sterling Lines

In Adam's office Finn unpacked the rucksack and gave the collected documents and biological samples to a military intelligence officer. Another officer took the iBOW and began downloading the pictures and data.

"Good work Finn, I'm impressed. The stuff you've returned with is invaluable," Mac praised.

Finn replied dryly, "Next time you can hike the sixty odd miles to get it, or provide a bloody vehicle!"

Mac patted him on the shoulder, "Sorry mate! Point taken. It was the only way to get you in there and avoid detection by the Russians. From what you discovered in the lab do you have a theory about what happened to cause the biological agent to be released?"

"I noticed lots of dead chemists, they died at their workstations. One of the bodies had a smashed test tube on the floor next to it. An explosion elsewhere in the facility destroyed part of the lab and the shock from the blast triggered the guy to drop it. It's obvious that the delivery device must've gone off accidentally. Most likely a rocket, developing a way to deliver the biological agent to their enemies' front door. They probably planned to test the weapon by sending it into the ocean or a remote island somewhere. That's what the superpowers did with nuclear weapons, it makes sense to think that they'd do the same with a biological one. The mistake was playing around with biological substances in the same building as explosives."

"Seems like a plausible conclusion Finn."

"What about that handprint? I'm certain that the person who left it behind took the biological weapon from the laboratory, they had a small case. Aren't you a little bit worried about that?"

"We're working on it. Hopefully we'll get a DNA match on the blood if the fingerprints draw a blank. To save time analysing the information I've relocated some of my military intelligence resources to this base. I've also put in a temporary transfer request for you to join my department. Adam's has already agreed to the request."

Finn looked at Adams, sitting behind his desk, "Thanks!"

"You're welcome." Adams said, with a smile on his face.

"So, what do you want me to do?" Finn said with a resigned air.

"In a nutshell, get the biological weapon back from whoever has taken it," Mac declared.

"And what about the Russians? Are you going to tell them about the bodies I found? We need to get those British soldiers returned home and arrange for proper burials. Their families need to be told that they've been found."

"Let's take things step by step Finn," Mac declared. "We can't do that without alerting them to the fact that we've been inside the exclusion zone. And we don't want to do that until we know that the biological weapon is safe, and in our hands."

"Well don't you forget about them, because I won't."

"Point taken," Mac confirmed.

❖ ❖ ❖ ❖

Finn paced up and down outside the briefing room. He looked at his watch for the fourth time in as many minutes. One of Mac's intelligence officers came out of the room and walked towards him, he stopped pacing and stared, waiting for some news. Instead, the officer just walked past him and down the hall towards the toilet. *Damn! How long does it take these guys to get some intel put together?*

Finn was still pacing around when the officer returned. He looked at Finn briefly before going back into the room.

Finn was about to give up and return to his quarters when the briefing room door suddenly opened. From inside Mac shouted blindly into the hall, "Finn! Get yourself in here…we've found something."

"It's about bloody time."

Finn entered the room and found Mac leaning over one of the intelligence officers who was working on a laptop.

"What have you found?" Finn enquired.

"Agneta Bergqvist!" Mac announced, while pointing at the computer screen.

Finn looked at the screen finding an Interpol web page with the image of a beautiful young woman with short blonde hair. He read details of an arrest for dealing ecstasy at a rave in Ibiza and a lenient judge giving her a suspended two-year sentence. He skimmed over the other details then began reading her personal description. Twenty-one years old, five foot seven tall and one hundred and fifteen pounds.

"She doesn't look like a hardened criminal to me Mac. Are you sure it was her?"

"That picture is twelve years old, She's thirty-three now. But I must admit I'm surprised with your response."

"Why?"

"Are you telling me that you've never heard of Agneta Bergqvist?"

"Should I have?" Finn said dismissively.

"It's no surprise to me! You don't get women like her in the Turks Head," Adams quipped.

"Very Funny! Go on Mac, tell me what I've missed then."

Mac told the operator to bring up a YouTube video. It showed the same woman, now older, speaking at a conference of some type.

"Pause it a second," Mac instructed, then picked up a piece of paper from the desk. He skimmed over the document and began reading out aloud, ad-libbing as he went, "Agneta Bergqvist daughter of Arvid Bergqvist, a Swedish billionaire who owns URMINA, a uranium mining company. He landed on his feet as a young geologist by discovering a massive deposit of the nuclear gold in the north of the country in what was then forestry land. He rounded up some investors and bought up all the land cheaply from the state. There have been a few allegations over the years that the deal involved corruption but no proof has surfaced. If it was a corrupt deal then it involved people all the way to the top. Once he'd secured the land and all the permits, he chopped the trees down and began mining. This was just around the time of the cold war when countries were going nuclear on everything, mostly weapons. Along with finding uranium he also discovered large deposits of iron ore which led to expanded mining operations. The guy has made a fortune. The old man is in his eighties now. He started a family in his fifties when he met his third, and current wife, Elise. A union which yielded two children. The first born, Bjorn, died at seventeen in a motorbike accident leaving his younger sister Agneta to inherit the lot."

"I'm still not convinced Mac. She's got no reason to steal a biological weapon," Finn observed.

"That's because you don't know what she's all about. Daddy's uranium mining doesn't sit well with someone who's the world's best-known environmentalist and climate activist. Chopping all those trees down and creating nuclear waste all over the planet is bad news to her. She's spent the last ten years setting up what has now become one of the biggest environment protection companies in the world, EXISTENCE. The business has over fifty million twitter followers, that's twenty more than POTUS has. Add to that over a hundred million YouTube subscribers and it tells you this woman knows her marketing. The business generates income from green product endorsements, charitable donations, and advertising. They've had over forty billion YouTube plays and every one of those plays generates revenue from sponsor adverts. She's a good business woman, brilliant in fact. Existence is now one of the richest companies in Europe."

"That's all-good Mac but she's already rich. Why would she go to all the trouble to set up this business?"

"That's easy Finn! She did it to stick two fingers up to her father and his environment damaging friends. The latest intel says that she hasn't spoken to the old man for over ten years. This is her speaking at the latest Green Planet Conference…Ok, play the video."

The computer operator pressed a key on the keyboard and turned up the volume.

"World leaders, politicians and scientists keep filling our heads with empty words. While they promise change, people are suffering, some are dying. Entire ecosystems have begun collapsing. We are at the start of the mass extinction of life on our planet. Two thousand species become extinct on the planet every year and all they can talk about is money and economic growth. For over thirty years environmental scientists have warned about the coming end to human, animal and plant life, unless we change our ways. Despite all the evidence, our leaders continue to look on and do nothing. They smile in our faces and lie behind our backs. Time is running out, to create change we need a revolution, a global revolution without borders or leaders. Plants and animals don't understand

borders, they get on with their lives. Trying to exist while humankind takes away their home, our home, Earth! Join our revolution, donate now online, if you cannot donate subscribe to our channel and follow the message as the story unfolds. Today we are bringing the revolution to our leaders, maybe then they'll listen."

The sound of the crowd applauding and cheering continued after the speech ended.

Mac ordered the operator to switch the video off and turned to Finn, "Does that sound like a threat to you? That stuff about a revolution and bringing the message to the world leaders. It sounds like one to me, especially now that we know what she's been up to."

"Shit!", Finn banged his fist on the desk. "I get it! She's got a point to prove."

"What do you mean?"

"Think Mac! What would you do if some guy doesn't listen to you? You show him what can happen to him if he doesn't start to."

"You mean…"

"By releasing that biological weapon somewhere on the planet to show what climate change is going to do. Wipe everything out! A small dose from a dropped test tube wiped out a town in Russia. If you consider what happened in a barren piece of land at the arse end of nowhere what could she do with her doomsday device in London, Paris, or New York. Just think of the devastation."

"What the F..." Mac held his words and walked away to the window, "She could wipe us all out in a second."

"Exactly!" Finn confirmed. "And forget about just arresting her. This woman is smart and a fast thinker, I discovered that first-hand in Russia. Before you arrest her, we need to know that the weapon is safe, how many test tubes she took, are they all accounted for, and then, and only then can we get to her."

Mac grabbed his jacket from a chair, "Adams, get me a helicopter! I need to get to London straight away with this information. Finn, stay here with the intel guys. See if you can think of a way to get to her without her knowing, that's what you're good at.

An hour after Mac had left Finn looked at the four agents sitting around the desk working on laptops, "Come on guys we need to speed things up a bit. I need to know everything about this woman and her Company. If we're going to find a way to get the weapon back without alerting her, we need to know her accessibility points. People and places that she trusts. Where she eats, how she travels, who she's sleeping with. I want to know everything!"

The intelligence officers continued working, daring not to speak.

"What about the two men who I encountered in the town? Have you matched the photos to anyone?" Finn demanded.

"I'm checking through her known associates. They post a lot of stuff online when doing environmental protests or rallies. We may get a match on someone who has been videoed or photographed with her," one announced.

"What about the mobile phones?"

Another replied, "I'm working on that sir, running a program to crack the passcode, it should be done within the hour."

"Thanks. Look guys the next few days are going to be stressful. We all need to work as a team. If you find anything useful, I need to know straight away."

Finn became impatient, feeling that the situation was getting away from him, beyond his control. He was relying on computers for information but a gun or fist was his normal way of persuasion. He could see that his impatience was starting to affect the intel officers. Finn recognised the signs, tiredness, and stress, eventually he announced, "Ok guys let's take a break, get yourselves down to the mess hall we'll pick this up again in an hour."

The intel officers did as he suggested and began chatting among themselves while they left the room. Now alone, Finn leaned back in a chair, closed his eyes and visualised the figure in black shooting at him. He imagined the beautiful woman from the Interpol image wearing the black uniform and carrying an assault rifle. He puzzled over what had turned a young woman into a potential terrorist with a cause worth dying for.

❖ ❖ ❖ ❖

Adams put the phone down, "It appears Mac liked you Finn. The people down in London have agreed with him that the best way to play this is a covert operation involving the least number of people as possible. If news gets out that a biological weapon has disappeared it will cause public panic…and the eco-terrorists will go to ground. He's on his way here to fill you in on what's been discussed."

"No problem. I assume this covert operation involves him sitting behind a desk while I'm out there somewhere getting shot at."

"That's what you signed up for Finn. You can always get you posted back to Afghanistan if you prefer."

Finn protested, "If you remember I returned here to get some well-deserved R & R."

Adams ignored the comment and looked at his watch, "Mac will be here within the hour."

"I'll check up on the intel guys, they may have found something we can work on."

Finn left Adams in his office and returned to the briefing room. The four military intelligence officers continued working on gathering intel, posting each new piece of information on the wall for the others to review.

Finn looked at the multiple images and documents, pointing at pictures of the two men that he'd killed, he asked, "Have you managed to identify these two men yet?"

One officer spoke, "I've just received details from Interpol on one. Nils Wallin, a thirty-four Swedish computer expert, caught hacking into the Swedish national banking system, and spent five years in prison. Released two years ago then he just disappeared off the grid."

"Until he decided to start playing about with satellite systems inside Russia, another bad career choice by him," Finn quipped. "And the other?"

"He appears in a lot of the news clippings and Existence YouTube videos. He was most likely a bodyguard, as he seems to have spent his time shadowing the Bergqvist woman. We would need to interview someone at the company to find out who he was."

"And alert them that we know about them? No chance. What about the woman?"

"She's unmarried, no boyfriend, or girlfriend, at least not one that is mentioned anywhere on the internet. She seems to be a bit of a loner. I called the head office in Stockholm, pretending to be a journalist wanting an interview with her. The man in charge of PR said he would tell her and she'll call me if she's interested. I can't find a home address for her other than the father's mansion in Stockholm. Given what Mac said she most likely has another home somewhere else."

Another intelligence officer interrupted, "Existence has bought large areas of land in the north of Sweden, mainly in Lapland, she could be living somewhere up there."

"Without an address it doesn't help us," Finn stated the obvious. "All we know is that this woman has a company with an office in Stockholm. So that is where we need to start."

"How's it going?" Mac announced as he walked into the room. Finn noticed the change of clothes, jeans, polo top, light sports jacket, and designer trainers.

"We've managed to get a lot of info but nothing that will join the dots. A dead IT expert, a dead bodyguard, a billionaire's daughter with an assault rifle, a missing biological weapon and a company that is based in Stockholm," Finn replied dryly.

"Then that's where we start!" Mac said excitedly.

"I've just said the same thing."

Mac grinned, "Like minds Finn."

"What's with the new dress code?"

"I'm coming with you. I've spoken to the authorities and presented the information from your Russia trip. They don't want news of a potential biological weapon threat getting out in the open so the team here, you, me and Adams is where the buck stops. Our task is simple, recover the weapon at all costs. They'll provide whatever we need in terms of equipment and money."

"You can start by getting me to Stockholm so I can get a good look at the Existence offices."

Mac walked over to an intelligence officer, "Get me the layout of the place."

The officer printed out some documents and handed them to Mac. The MI6 agent studied the plans then spread them out on the table, "Okay Finn this is what we've got." Mac pointed to the details on the document while talking, "The company occupies the top two floors of what looks like a typical five storey office building near Berzelii park.

It's near the waterfront and marina. The lower floors below Existence are occupied by a legal firm, then a web design company and finally a PR agency."

He stopped and turned to the officer, "What do we know about those businesses?"

The officer replied, "Nothing suspicious, all seem to be legit."

Mac continued, "The Existence office on the fourth floor appears to be mainly admin people. The top floor looks interesting, it has a balcony, it may be an apartment."

"Maybe Bergqvist uses that as a base when she's in town," Finn said.

"And you would like to get in there and take a closer look," Mac added.

"If it's an admin building it may just be a front to cover up what's really going on inside the Company. They'll still need to behave like a normal business with records of employees, their wages, benefits etc. They must present annual accounts and tax returns. To do that they must raise invoices and purchase orders. The bank payments related to those transactions will leave a digital trail somewhere, most likely stored somewhere on site. If I can get inside, I may be able to pick up some intel that will lead us directly to her. Finding her has to be our top priority as she was the last person seen with the biological weapon."

"Sounds like a logical place to start, when do you want to go?"

Finn grabbed his leather jacket from a chair, "Now!"

Chapter 7
AkkaJaure Lake, Lapland

Agneta Bergqvist, sitting on the porch of her converted hunting lodge, looked out over Akkajaure Lake. The vast expanse of water was the result of the Government damming the Lule River in nineteen twenty-three to provide fuel for the hydroelectric plant inside the dam. The power station now provided green energy to the surrounding areas. The hydroelectric power station proved to her that humanity and nature could live together in harmony by using use the resources of the planet sustainably. She told herself that building the dam justified the sacrifice of some land and trees.

The midnight sun was hovering over the horizon, casting twilight across the lake. The mild summer wind produced waves for the last sunbeams to dance upon. She took comfort from the knowledge that no other human could enjoy the beauty and tranquillity her land provided, from the winter snows when the lake would freeze, to the summer sun that brought the reindeer migration.

She tapped the silver briefcase with her foot and reflected on the previous day's events. The loss of Nils and Patrik, close friends since meeting up and sharing interests at university, weighed on her mind. They'd planned the mission to secure the biological weapon to the finest detail, including travelling to the area annually for the last five years, taking great risks to get behind the Russian defences. Once the signs of new plant growth began to appear, they'd collectively agreed to release the dogs. Despite the possibility that they may die, it would be a small sacrifice for a greater cause. The tracking devices worn by the dogs allowed them to remotely see how they migrated through the area. The dogs had even begun living in the ruins of the town. They decided together, with the dogs still alive after eight months, that it would be safe to enter the exclusion zone.

It had taken another year to secure the equipment and technical expertise to access the satellite. She'd lost count of the numerous bribes she'd given to Russian officials to secure the access codes for the satellite.

All their patience and planning had paid off. They'd secured the weapon but Nils and Patrik would miss the victory parade.

She poured a large glass of vodka and downed it in one then saluted her fallen comrades with the empty glass. As she stretched her arm the pain from the bullet wound in her shoulder returned. Her private physician had completed the work of stitching her up, finding no major or lasting damage. The pain made her think of the man who had shot her. Very quick on his feet, fast reactions and deadly with either his hands or a gun. The sort of man that she needed in her organisation. Someone that she could trust and depend upon.

She picked up her satellite phone and made a call, "Lars, did you recover our friends' bodies?"

"We gave them a burial at sea as you requested. The killer took their personal items and mobile phones."

"Don't worry about that, they won't be able to use the phones to trace us, they only used them to communicate with each other. More importantly, what have you found out about the person who killed our colleagues?"

"I've checked with our contacts around Europe, so far no one has come up with anything that indicates anything official. It's more likely they were civilians checking the place over or trying to claim notoriety for getting inside first. We've heard of people trying unsuccessfully in the past. The price of seeking fame and glory."

"You keep saying 'They', I only encountered one man."

"There must've been at least two of them."

"Why do you say that?" Agneta hissed.

"Because they also robbed the bank. They took the contents in the safety deposit boxes, no cash, old bank notes would be worthless now but still traceable. They'll have taken gold, silver, gems, jewellery, things that they can sell on the black market."

"You're now saying that they're thieves?"

"I don't know for sure but the Russians have worried about looters for years. The ones who tried in the past paid the ultimate price. These guys were the lucky ones, but you can understand why they did it, there's a lot of valuable items left inside the town."

"I think you're wrong. The person who killed both Nils and Patrik was a trained killer, possibly military or ex-military at least. Do you have any way to find out where they're from?"

"Like I said so far, all I know is that it wasn't official but you could be right, other countries could be interested outside of our sources. The US, UK or someone from China or the Middle East, however, there's no intel suggesting that's the case."

"Keep looking!" Agneta barked. "We need to find these people to confirm their intentions. They'll pay for killing our friends and interfering in our plans. If you think they're just a group of opportunist thieves then they'll need to find a way to turn what they took into cash. As you've already said, they can only do that by using sources on the black market. Do we have any contacts that handle stolen jewellery or bullion who we can use to help trace the thieves?"

"I'll get some of my men working on it. We've got contacts in a lot of the local police networks. They may be able to point us to someone who would do that kind of thing. We know there's no honour among thieves. If we offer them money they'll quickly inform on their closest friends."

"Stay on it. I want results quickly."

"Of course."

"Did you finalise the meeting with the Indian engineer?"

"Yes, he's agreed to work with us. He's now on route to Början as we speak. He doesn't know the full extent of the work required. As a guarantee to ensure he does what we want I can use the threat of violence to his wife and daughter as leverage. I'll inform him of the requirements of the job when he's on site, and the penalties for failure."

"Good. Call me when you've got everything set up at the base. Don't let anyone in your team become complacent, we've got a mission to complete, I don't want any problems. Until we find these thieves, we need to be careful. They know that other people were at the research facility and may try to trace us."

"Okay, bye."

Bergqvist hung up the call and threw her mobile down on the table. She lifted the silver case up onto her lap and snapped open the latches. She slowly opened the lid revealing seven small test tubes secured in the specially shaped foam interior. Each tube sealed with a metal cap, ensuring the bluish liquid inside could not leak out. She touched the empty slot, the space for the eighth test tube which she'd seen smashed on the laboratory floor. Taking one tube out she shook it and watched the liquid wash about inside. As she held the tube up to the failing light, she imagined the death contained inside. After several moments she replaced the tube and locked the case.

She drank more vodka and stared at the beauty of the nature surrounding her and considered the action that she was about to take, how she had fought for years to get the world leaders to see sense but now on the verge of making a decision that would destroy thousands of human and animal lives. She felt some remorse. The destruction of whole ecosystems and the earth would become a wasteland at her hands. She justified her decision knowing that after fifty years or so life would return but without the ever-growing human population to destroy it. A small sacrifice to make in the four billion years of the earth's existence.

Her emotions changed to hate. She thought of her father and his actions that had led to the destruction of life on many levels, from the trees he had cut down in the Swedish wilderness to the radiation poisoned beaches of many remote pacific islands. The wealth that he had amassed over the years had an environmental cost that she was unable to make him see.

Without his support she had managed to create her own wealth. He did have his uses like fooling him into selling the disused iron ore mine to Existence for just a dollar. It had been easy convincing him it would raise his profile being involved in the environmentalist cause.

She knew her father did not care about the environment. It was just a good PR move to help push up the share price while benefiting from a tax write off for Urmina. Little did he know that Början would become the place where life in a new world would evolve, without nations and borders, or him.

She moved inside, the cold evening air making her chilly. She placed the small metal case inside the safe, walked to the bedroom and fell asleep.

Chapter 8
Helsinki, Finland

Petrikov walked into the jewellery shop in Helsinki centre still brimming with pride at pulling off the task. In his right hand he grasped three ruby and diamond necklaces. His internet research informed him that similar items currently changing hands for sums more than fifty thousand euros. He approached the glass counter and stared at the jewellery trays, ignoring the young sales assistant when she asked if he needed help. He knew she would not be able to help him get what he wanted. For that he needed the owner who was currently trying to convince a young woman to buy some earrings.

Petrikov moved further along the glass counter, making sure to interrupt the negotiations by invading the customer's space. Feeling uncomfortable at the large scruffily dressed man standing next to her the young woman made her excuses, put down the earrings, and quickly left the shop.

The owner sighed at the loss of a potential sale and began to replace the earring samples under the counter, "Can I help you?"

Petrikov looked up, proud of his work, "Don't worry my friend, the loss of a fifty Euro sale will soon be forgotten once you see what I've got for you."

The man's expression changed to one of intrigue, "Which is?"

Petrikov gently laid the necklaces on the counter, "These!"

The jeweller fitted a magnifying eyeglass to his left eye and studied the quality of the gems. He completed the process by checking each of the jewellery items twice. Once complete, he stared at the items for a moment then said, "You're looking to sell these?"

"That's the general idea," Petrikov replied impatiently. "Are you interested or not?"

"Sir, I estimate that these items are from the late nineteenth century. They're not the sort of thing that a man dressed like yourself would bring to my shop. Therefore, I must ask, are they stolen?"

"Of course not!" Petrikov snatched the jewellery items from the counter, stuffed them into his coat pocket and moved towards the door.

"Wait!" the jeweller protested.

Petrikov stopped and turned round to face the man.

After several moments of silence the jeweller said, "Come with me," and lifted the counter top, allowing Petrikov access to the other side. He guided the Russian through a doorway into a small room with a table and four chairs, then nervously asked, "How much do you want for them?"

"Sixty thousand euros."

"You're joking, they have no value to me unless I remove the stones. The police will arrest me if I try to sell them in their current condition. This collection disappeared in the nineteen thirties, presumed stolen. Now you appear in my shop eighty years later wanting to sell them. Tell me the truth, where did you get them?"

"An inheritance from a dead relative."

The jeweller laughed, "You expect me to believe that a member of your family has died leaving these jewels behind for you? No, I cannot deal with these items if they're stolen, please take them and leave."

"Okay! Just give me twenty thousand and I'll forget your insult."

The jeweller thought for a moment, weighing up his options, "Ten!"

"Fine...but if I find out you've robbed me, I'll be back to collect the difference."

Petrikov handed the jewellery over and received his payment. Leaving the shop, he considered his next move. He now had enough money for a flight to the US. There he could sell the rest of his haul without the hassle.

❖ ❖ ❖ ❖

The jeweller watched the man leave, then made a phone call, "Matis, I've just had a customer, a Russian man, who's looking to sell some items from the Rasmus collection."

"The Rasmus collection? Are you sure? The collection was reported as lost in Russia many years ago, presumed stolen, broken up or stored in a private collection."

"I'm very sure. I've got some of the items here."

"You bought the items from this man?"

"Of course! At only ten thousand euros it was an irresistible bargain. But that's not why I'm calling you. I'm sure that he's got the rest of the collection somewhere. They'll now be worth a fortune. You've got the resources that can relieve him of the burden. I've got the skills required to remove the gems and a list of customers willing to buy. Between us we can realise their true value. Are you interested in a fifty-fifty partnership?"

"I like your proposal. Where's this man now?"

"I've sent my assistant Hilla to follow him, to find out where he goes and where he's staying."

"That's a good idea. I'll be there soon so we can discuss this opportunity face to face."

∴ ∴ ∴ ∴

Petrikov felt hungry and couldn't allow himself to miss the opportunity to sample the local food. He stopped at a bar, ate, then continued drinking until the early evening. He enjoyed the local beers washed down with glasses of Finnish vodka. He paid his bar tab in cash, visited the toilet, then stumbled out of the doorway into the street. Hilla watched from over the road. He staggered drunkenly down the road, knocking over a bin as he went. Hilla crossed over and walked a few metres behind him.

At the entrance to the hotel Petrikov barged into some leaving guests, causing an argument. After swearing loudly in Russian, he staggered inside and demanded his room key from the woman receptionist. He staggered up the staircase using the bannister to hold himself up. Hilla watched from the pavement outside. At his room door he fumbled with the key, focusing his eyes on the key slot. After several failed attempts, he managed to turn the key in the lock. The door sprung open and he fell inside. He pushed himself up from the floor, kicked the door shut and dived on the bed. After a few moments staring at the ceiling, he picked up the phone. He called room service and ordered a bottle of vodka.

"Excuse me," Hilla asked. "What's the room number of the drunken man who has just entered?"

"I'm sorry, but we don't give out the details of our guests," the receptionist remarked.

"Please, he's my father, I'm worried about him. He's had an argument with my mother and she's kicked him out. He lost his job and now he only cares about drinking."

After checking that her boss was not near the receptionist whispered, "Two zero three."

"Thank you."

Hilla went up the stairs, waited for several minutes on the landing then returned downstairs to the reception, "I think he's asleep now. I'll return tomorrow."

Hilla walked into the jewellery store finding Matis standing behind the counter with the owner. The two men stopped talking and looked at her. Matis approached her with the same menacing look in his eyes that she had endured many times before. She smelt his rancid breath as he got up close to her.

"What did you discover? Talk girl!" Matis snapped, grabbing her arm as he spoke.

"He's staying at the Regent Hotel, room two zero three."

"What's he been doing? You've been gone for over three hours," the jeweller barked.

"He was drinking at a bar in the city, now he's very drunk. I checked at the room door, he's sleeping now, snoring like a pig."

Matis let go of her arm, "Good, very good. I like you. You've got spirit." A perverted grin appeared on his face as he turned to the jeweller, "This young woman is wasted working here with you in this shop. Send her to my club tomorrow."

Hilla shivered at the thought and moved behind the counter, seeking refuge.

The owner touched her behind, "Not before I sample the goods one more time."

Matis laughed, "Enjoy my good friend. Now I've got business to arrange."

Hilla watched as Matis left the shop and got into his car. The owner wrapped his arm around her waist and pushed her towards the small room.

As the car pulled away into the evening traffic Matis took out mobile phone and dialled the number...

Chapter 9
Början, Lapland

As the SUV struggled on the dry earth the Indian design engineer looked out of the window and considered his decision. The seven-hour flight from Dubai to Stockholm, coupled with the two-hour onward flight to Kiruna and an hour in the SUV, had left him tired and weary. He wiped sweat from his forehead then looked around at the three-armed men sharing the journey. He was unsure if their job was to protect him or to keep him prisoner. He stared out of the passenger side window and began to feel uncomfortable.

The SUV continued up the side of the mountain, the main tarmac road now thirty minutes behind them. The engineer looked at his mobile, *no signal.*

The SUV finally stopped at a large steel gate. The driver lowered the window, punched a code into a keypad and the gate began to open. The SUV moved inside and the gate closed silently. The SUV pulled into a flattened parking area, cut out of the mountainside. The driver parked alongside several unmarked white four-wheel drive vehicles. In front of the parking area there was a large steel door built into the mountainside. Made from two sections, covering an area thirty feet high and fifty feet wide. Built into the large right door was a smaller, standard size door.

The voice from behind shouted, "We're here, get your stuff."

The driver and his colleagues climbed out of the vehicle and headed towards the small steel door. The Indian engineer grabbed his case and followed. The thick steel door opened hydraulically and a tall man with long blonde hair tied in a ponytail, greeted them, "You're here at last."

The guards disappeared inside, leaving the blonde-haired man with the engineer, "Mr Molantra, welcome to Början. I'm Lars, come inside."

Lars pressed a red button on the wall and the door shut behind them. Molantra walked into a carved-out tunnel that led into the distance. He imagined it was a mine of some type. Lined up along one side of the tunnel there was a row of new SUVs, trucks, diggers, off road buggies and motorbikes. The guards climbed into a battery powered four-wheel drive buggy, similar in size to a golf cart.

"Come, get on board and I'll show you the facility," Lars instructed.

With everyone on board the driver set off down the tunnel. After a drive of five minutes, they stopped at a concrete structure which blocked the tunnel with a single door in the middle, providing access to whatever lay beyond. The men climbed out of the buggy and proceeded to the door. Lars entered a code and the door opened. He turned to Molantra and gestured for him to enter.

On the other side the Indian engineer found himself in a chamber. Once everyone was inside Lars shut the door, steam jets filled the cavity and surrounded them. After a pause a large fan drew the steam out of the chamber into the outer tunnel.

"Decontamination. We don't want any foreign bodies inside the facility," Lars explained.

Inside Molantra found an ultra-modern facility with the main tunnel split into seven separate ones, leading in different directions. The original rock walls replaced by a mixture of stainless steel and plastic, giving the facility a futuristic look. Above each of the tunnels an illuminated sign indicated the destination, Archives, Stores, Biosphere, Accommodation, IT, Security and Research.

"This will be your home until you complete the agreed assignment. You'll spend most of your time in the Research and Accommodation sections. I can assure you that the Research sector has the latest equipment to help you in your task. There's also a team of highly trained scientists ready to assist you. The Accommodation sector has everything you will need when you're not working; your personal room, a canteen, recreation area, a gym, swimming pool and spa. You'll find that life will be very comfortable here." Lars announced.

"What is this place?" Molantra asked.

"At Existence we've taken the decision to protect the life that exists on our planet before it's gone forever. We've created this facility, which we call Början, to store seeds and the embryos of life that have evolved here over billions of years. The seeds of plants, from grasses to trees, from fruits to vegetables and the DNA of living creatures, saving them for future generations to enjoy."

As they walked through the tunnel towards the accommodation sector Lars continued to explain, "We've set up this place as an experiment in human living, protected from the environment outside and fully self-sufficient. We've got our own energy and food sources so if an extinction level event happens outside, we can survive in here for up to two years. The people you see are volunteers. They have given up all their property for the cause and have cut ties with their families and friends. Soon we'll start a new beginning with humans and the other species on the planet living together in a symbiotic way, not one creature destroying all the others for greed..." Lars stopped himself realising he was beginning to rant, a symptom of the environmentalist cause. "Sorry, I sometimes get carried away. You're not here to worry about that stuff. You're here for a specific job."

Lars showed the engineer to his living quarters. After a brief tour of the accommodation block and a walk to the research sector he arrived at the laboratory where he was to work. The engineer met the other scientists chosen to work alongside him, experts in chemistry, physics, biology, and electronics. He noted the look on each of their faces when he shook their hands, a mixture of nervousness and fear.

Unable to contain himself any longer Molantra asked, "What exactly is it that you want me to create for you? In Dubai they offered a fixed fee contract in return for designing a chemical delivery system for agriculture. No one mentioned that I would be held underground in a secure facility."

Lars responded curtly, "Maybe you should've asked! If I remember you spent the time negotiating the price."

"I'm not sure that I'll be able to help you. I'm sorry but it appears that I've wasted your time. Can you please return me to the airport?"

Lars pulled out his pistol and aimed it at Molantra's head, "You made an agreement. The boss doesn't like it when people break their agreements. You've got two options. I can terminate your contract now or you can start getting on with the work you've agreed to do. Which option do you prefer?"

Molantra said hesitantly, "Okay, please put it away. Don't worry I'll do as you ask. Can you start by explaining exactly what it is that you need?"

"Think of your work on crop dusting equipment. We've formulated a new biological agent that requires dilution into a higher volume solution for dispersal over a wider area in the form of a gas or mist. The dispersal device that you're going to create must be remotely operated, compact, and easily transportable. The chemist will formulate the solution based on your requirements for the delivery device. As part of our agreement, we've provided you with everything you need to be successful, a modern facility with technology, equipment, and personnel. Once you complete the delivery device you will be paid and taken to the airport." Lars toyed with the pistol in his hand and added, "You know the cost of failure."

"What's the purpose of the biological agent that you want us to work with? Is it a new kind of pesticide?" Molantra asked.

A wry grin appeared on Lars's face, "I like that description. Yes, it's a new kind of pesticide. Now get on with your work, time is running out."

❖ ❖ ❖ ❖

Disturbed by the ringing, Agneta Bergqvist picked up her mobile phone and answered abruptly, "Lars!"

"Boss, the engineer is on site and he's been given his orders. When do you plan to bring the biological agent?"

"I'll come in a few days. You need to step up the process of finalising the facility. We need to be able to start our plans within the next few weeks."

"One of our contacts in Finland has been told of a man selling vintage Russian jewellery. He's staying at a hotel in Helsinki. It could be the thieves, what do you want me to do?

"Go there and find out who he is, who he works for and why he was at Yacheyka. And don't forget to find out who he was with. And be careful, if it's the man I met he's quick on his feet and deadly."

"I'll leave straight away. Do you have any objection to the local contact keeping the jewellery? It's part of the negotiation."

"I don't want it. It has no value to me and very soon it will have none to him either."

Chapter 10
Existence Office, Stockholm

The small executive jet landed at a municipal airport on the outskirts of Stockholm, with Mac and Finn the only passengers. Using forged papers, they breezed through security and picked up an airport hire car. The woman at the counter took an interest in Finn which made the process quicker.

They arrived in the city centre an hour later where Mac parked in an underground car park and the two men headed on foot to the Existence offices. Standing near the entrance Mac spotted a museum on the other side of the road that looked onto the office block, "Let's get in there and see if we can find a vantage point to recon this building."

Finn nodded in agreement, "Good idea."

They entered the museum and wandered around the exhibits acting like tourists, gradually making their way to the upper floor where Finn spotted a maintenance door that headed to the roof. Using Mac, who was admiring a presentation on abstract art, as cover, Finn picked the lock and moved quickly inside. He rushed along a maintenance corridor until he discovered a room with a small window that led out onto the roof. He pushed the window open and crawled out onto the leaded roof.

He pulled binoculars from his brown leather jacket and scanned the office building on the other side of the road. The top floor appeared to be unoccupied with no lights or appliances switched on. The open plan apartment had a woman's touch with modern furniture and decor. The layout consisted of a bedroom, open plan kitchen and large living area. The living area layout included large sliding glass doors that led onto a balcony with chairs, tables and plant pots with bushes.

He looked for security measures and noticed a camera on the roof edge looking down onto the balcony. Having found one he assumed that there would be more inside the building. He continued his review moving to the area above the apartment, finding a machine room for the lift, storage tanks for water and the heating system exhaust outlet.

Below the apartment he observed an office containing several members of staff sitting at desks, working.

Confident that he had enough information on the layout of the premises Finn returned to Mac who asked, "Any joy? What did you find?"

"There's definitely an apartment above the office. It looks like no one is currently home. A perfect opportunity for us to do some snooping about."

"I'm all for that as long as we do it covertly, I don't want any run ins with local law enforcement."

Finn looked at his watch, "It's sixteen hundred hours, they'll soon be locking up for the night, come on let's get moving."

The two men left the museum and returned to the street outside where Finn said, "You stay with the car. If I'm not back by nineteen hundred hours then assume something has gone wrong and you'll have to decide what to do."

"Are you going to fill me in with your plan?"

Without answering Finn set off running, crossed the road and down the side of the Existence office building. He spotted the entrance to the underground carpark. Alongside there was an area for storing rubbish bins and a maintenance door that someone had wedged open.

Finn grinned when he discovered how a member of staff had overridden the complex security system with just a brick. He watched as the carpark attendant checked the details of cars entering. At an opportune moment he ran up the maintenance ramp and in through the open door. He walked slowly along the corridor and found the car park elevator. He pressed the button to call the lift, hiding behind a car while waiting. The lift doors opened showing it unoccupied. He moved from behind the car, inside the lift and found the service hatch on the ceiling. After banging the panel open, he reached up and pulled himself onto the top of the lift carriage.

Hanging down into the lift he pressed the top floor button and closed the hatch. From his vantage point on the top of the lift he waited as it gradually moved upwards. At the top floor he jumped off into the lift motor room. Almost instantly the lift returned to the lower floors.

Finn broke the lock on the door and made his way out onto the roof.

He found the security camera and slowly turned the head so that it pointed away from the door that led out onto the balcony, creating a blind spot.

Happy that he would now be able to proceed undetected he dropped down onto the balcony. He tried the door, finding it unlocked and slowly slid it open. Entering the room, he listened for activity elsewhere in the property then gently closed the door behind him. Large modern furniture filled the main living room but nothing that the owner would use to store documents. He edged his way slowly past the open plan kitchen and into a corridor. On his left there was a large bathroom with a walk-in shower, sauna, and a large hot tub style bath. He walked into the small bedroom on his right and began checking the wardrobes and cupboards, finding women's clothes and shoes, but nothing to identify the owner.

Further down the corridor he found the main entrance door and a small broom cupboard with a few coats. Beyond the hallway there was another larger, master, bedroom. Finn walked in and moved to the wardrobe. Sliding open the doors he found more women's clothes and shoes. He closed the doors and looked around the room. Above the bed there was a large print of an idyllic landscape with a small cabin and a lake. Finn took a photo of the print using his iBOW. He lifted the print down from the wall and laid it face down on the bed. Stuck to the rear he found a label with a serial number and the words 'AkkaJaure, Bergqvist.' Finn took a picture of the label then replaced the print on the wall.

As he began leaving the master bedroom Finn heard footsteps outside on the other side of the entrance door. He stepped back into the bedroom with one eye on the door. He heard some voices, a key in the lock and the door suddenly opened. He assumed that he had tripped a security device, maybe a pressure pad on the floor or maybe a magnetic switch on the wardrobe doors. He now found himself cut off from the corridor and his escape route to the roof.

Finn froze as he watched two men armed with pistols walk past him and move down the corridor towards the living room. He considered escaping via the front door but before he could move one of the men turned towards the bedroom.

Finn hid behind the door. As the man entered, he grabbed him around the neck with his left arm while covering his mouth with his right hand. The man struggled and Finn used all his strength in a choke manoeuvre, knocking him unconscious. He pulled the body further into the room and hid it on the far side of the bed.

Taking a quick look outside the doorway to confirm the other man was in the main living room, Finn edged out of the bedroom and into the hall. He opened the main entrance door, walked out onto a landing, and shut the door gently behind himself. He proceeded down the small landing, noticing a staircase on his left and a lift directly in front. Using the lift would alert other security guards so he chose the stairs. He looked at his watch, *17.32*.

He moved down the first few stairs, slowly checking for security cameras on the walls below. Seeing a camera pointing down on the next landing, ready to catch anyone coming up the stairs, he stayed close to the wall until he was directly under the camera. His only option was to disable it so he ripped the wires out of the wall.

The security monitor in the lobby displayed the separate camera images in rotation. The image of a snowy screen came and went while the guard was chatting to a woman who was leaving work.

Finn continued to edge down the stairs until he reached a door, the fire escape for the Existence office on the other side. He pushed the bar on the door and slowly walked inside. The light from several computer screens, left on by the users in a rush to get home, dimly lit the room. He wandered between the desks and noticed a glass partitioned room. *The computer server room.*

He tried the door finding it locked, cursed, then began picking the lock when a voice shouted something in Swedish. He dived onto the floor between some desks and rolled over onto his side. He looked along the floor and discovered a set of legs. *The man from upstairs.*

He watched as the man began walking towards him, stopping periodically to check where Finn was. As he approached Finn positioned himself under a desk. The man walked past and Finn reached out and pulled his legs away. The man fell forward, banging his hand against a desk and dropping the gun. The man quickly launched himself up onto all fours, then his feet, before spinning around to face

Finn who was now standing. They both looked at the gun. The man moved for it and Finn hit him with his right fist, knocking the man backwards. Finn advanced as the man stumbled, landing a quick left and another right. The force of the blows stunned the man, a cut appeared above his eyebrow and his nose bent at a strange angle.

Anger welled in the man and he rushed Finn, who sidestepped the advance and landed a powerful right blow directly onto his temple. The man fell forward, out cold, hitting the floor. Finn kicked the lifeless body then picked up the gun and stuffed it into his belt.

Finn continued to pick the lock on the server room door. Eventually, the lock sprung open and he walked inside discovering racks of hard drives and cables. *Where's a computer nerd when you need one?*

He looked around the room and found a series of numbers written on the wall, unsure of their relevance he took photos with the iBOW. *The intel guys can work out if it's important or not.*

He looked at his watch, 18.19. Realising time was running out he found the hard drive furthest away from the door and inserted a USB stick containing a virus that would allow the intel team to hack into the server from outside.

As he left the room, he pulled out random network cables and swapped them over into other sockets. A grin appeared on his face. *Bet they spend hours trying to find out what's wrong.*

He returned to the upstairs apartment and exited the way he had arrived via the lift motor room and the ground floor maintenance door.

He found the hire car in the underground car park and climbed into the passenger seat. Mac looked at his watch and said, "Sixteen fifty-two, talk about cutting it fine, did you find anything."

"I hope so but can we get out of here first?"

"No problem," Mac announced, before starting the engine and beginning the journey back to the airport. After returning the hire car, where Finn also picked up the Swedish woman's number, they returned to the exec jet and flew back to Sterling Lines.

❖ ❖ ❖ ❖

The guard in the apartment bedroom gasped, drawing air into his lungs. He could still feel the pressure around his neck and how his attacker had nearly squeezed the life from his body.

He got up off the floor and took the radio from his belt, "Agvald, are you there?" He released the talk button and waited for a response that did not come. He repeated the request, "Agvald, are you there?" Still no response, in desperation he called again, "Front desk are you there?"

"Go ahead."

"We've got an intruder on floor five, secure the building. Agvald is missing."

The radio fell silent and the guard returned to the task of looking for the intruder. After making sure the apartment was clear he made his way down to the lower floor and the office. He called out again on the radio, "Agvald, come in." In the distance he heard his own voice. He continued to speak, getting closer to the source of the sound and discovered Agvald's radio under a desk. He looked between the rows of desks and found the unconscious body of his battered companion.

After checking, and finding a weak pulse, he made another radio call, "Front desk, get an ambulance straight away, Agvald's in a bad way. We're looking for more than one person because they've given him a true beating."

❖ ❖ ❖ ❖

The security chief reported the incident involving the intruders to Lars. Unsure of what to do he made the call, "Agneta."

"Yes, Lars."

"We had a break in at the offices in Stockholm. Nothing appears to have been taken but two security guards were beaten up."

"They must've broken in for a reason, you need to keep looking. Do you have anything to indicate the who it was?"

"We caught one of the intruders on CCTV when he left the parking garage. The quality is poor, you can only get a glimpse of him. I'm sending the footage to you now."

Agneta's phone beeped and she put the call on hold while she watched the video. She gasped as it showed a man running down the maintenance corridor in jeans and a brown leather jacket. Despite the poor image quality, she recognised how the person moved, she had seen it before. She unlocked the call, "It's him, the man from Yacheyka. How did he trace us?"

"I don't know. I will..." Lars could not finish the sentence because Agneta had already cut him off. She cursed to herself and threw the phone onto the table.

Chapter 11
Regent Hotel, Helsinki

Petrikov rolled over on the bed, laid on his back and began staring at the ceiling. A thumping pressure filled his head. He looked to the bedside table and the half empty bottle of vodka. The digital clock radio showed a time of 10:23.

After showering and changing his clothes he sat on the bed and stared at the haul of jewels, gold, and cash. He fumbled through the items of jewellery until he found what he was looking for. With a sense of pride at his achievement he picked up the item and stared at it, then turned it over so he could read the inscription and confirm its ownership.

His attention moved to the subject of food, his stomach empty and queasy from minor alcohol poisoning. Realising that he had missed the hotel breakfast schedule he ordered room service instead.

❖ ❖ ❖ ❖

Lars stepped off the plane at Helsinki airport, following a five-hour flight from Kiruna with a stopover in Stockholm. After clearing customs, he proceeded to the exit and waited for Matis to arrive. The intel report on the man had made Lars cringe with disgust, he studied the picture before hiding it in his pocket.

The rain stopped and the morning sun broke through the clouds as a large black sedan, a relic of the communist era, pulled up at the curb alongside him. Looking inside he discovered an old man, in his late sixties, sitting on the back seat. The picture confirmed the passenger as Matis, accompanied by a bodyguard and driver.

The bodyguard climbed out of the front passenger side and spoke, "Are you Lars?"

The Swede nodded and the bodyguard opened the rear door. The old man leaned forward and spoke, "Come inside my friend, I'm Matis, how was your flight?"

Lars replied curtly, showing no respect for the local crime lord, "Tiresome! Take me to the Hotel."

The response upset Matis but he held his tongue, thinking of the haul of jewels instead, "Drive!"

The driver stepped on the accelerator and the big car lurched forward and headed out of the airport, towards the city.

Now calmed, Matis turned to Lars, "I hope we can complete our business in a courteous way."

"I'm not here to be your friend. I find your presence disgusting but it serves a purpose to an end. Let's get things wrapped up quickly, then we will go our separate ways. Tell me about the jewels and the seller."

"Very well. He visited an associate of mine with vintage jewels for sale. He sold some of them for a fraction of their true value. When I heard that someone was looking for Russian jewels coming onto the market, I got in touch. You've made your feelings clear, let me do the same. As I told you on the phone, our agreement is that you get the seller, I get the jewels."

Lars looked at the large bodyguard who had turned around to stare at him, "Fine, whatever you want, tell me about the jewels."

"They're part of a Russian jewellery collection created in the late nineteenth century, the Rasmus collection. A series of necklaces, bracelets, earrings and rings with diamonds and rubies set in gold. They disappeared from the market in the nineteen thirties, presumed stolen and broken up."

. "Good, we're talking about antique Russian jewellery that has been unseen for years. It appears you've found what I'm looking for but tell me more about who owned them last?"

"A scientist, a member of the old Russian elite."

"And what happened to this scientist?"

"He worked for the state both before and after the second world war doing biological research. He disappeared from public records sometime in the nineteen sixties."

Lars processed the information. *If the man at the hotel was not the person at Yacheyka then he must at least know who was.*

He sat quietly, staring out of the window as the car drove through the busy city streets. He watched the pedestrians and traffic whilst considering his options.

After a journey of thirty-eight minutes the car pulled up outside the Regent Hotel.

"We're here!" Matis declared.

Lars instructed, "We'll go in together with your bodyguard but I'll do all of the talking."

The three men entered the lobby. Matis approached the reception desk, placing a bank note on the counter top, "I've got a meeting with a friend, we don't want to be disturbed."

The receptionist quickly stuffed the hundred euro note into her pocket.

The men walked up the staircase onto the second-floor landing as the waiter appeared from the service elevator.

"Which room is that for?" Matis asked.

The waiter felt intimidated by the three men and mumbled, "203."

"Good timing, we'll take it for you. Here's a tip," Matis stuffed a fifty euro note in the young man's top pocket. "And I don't need to remind you that you've never seen us."

The young man nodded and rushed back to the elevator.

The abrupt knock at the door caught Petrikov off guard, "Yes!"

"Room service."

Forgetting his training, still groggy from the alcohol, he unhooked the security chain and unlocked the door.

The first punch broke his nose. He fell backwards and banged his elbow on the bed frame, causing a searing pain in his arm. He landed on his back as the large bodyguard crouched down and added two more heavy blows to his face. The bodyguard lifted him up onto a chair as he spat out a mouthful of blood and three of his teeth. He watched as they spun along the tiled floor. Dazed and confused from the blows, he looked around through blurred eyes. In the doorway he noticed two more men entering the room, shutting the door behind them.

The bodyguard fixed his gaze on the stash of loot on the bed as he moved to the corner of the room. For a moment he considered killing the others and taking it for himself. He quickly dismissed the thought as the image of his wife and two children butchered flashed into his mind.

"Take the stuff then leave us, we've got private business to discuss," Lars ordered.

Matis did not need to hear the offer twice, he pushed the jewellery items into the rucksack and left the room with the bodyguard in close attendance.

Lars punched Petrikov twice, once in the face and a second into his stomach. The force of the blow blew the air out of his lungs and he again slumped forward on the chair. Another series of blows landed on the Russian's face and torso. Lars moved behind the slumped body and pulled the head backwards almost snapping the neck.

Petrikov gave out a groan as Lars snarled, "The jewels! Where did you get them?"

Petrikov began to choke on the blood from his nose and mouth running down his throat.

Lars used his free hand to slap the Russian's face, "Speak!"

Between gasps for air Petrikov muttered, "I found them."

"You found them?" Lars increased the pressure on the head and neck, "Speak! It's your last chance to live."

"I found them in the wilderness…in Russia."

The comment surprised Lars and he released the pressure slightly, "Say that again."

"I found them in an old hunting cabin. There was a man's body there. Some wild dogs killed him…they tore him to pieces…his misfortune led to me finding my fortune."

"When did this happen?"

"Two days ago."

Lars paused for thought, unsure if the Russian was lying or telling the truth, "What is your name pig?"

"Alexandri Sudov."

Lars used his free hand to enter the details into his mobile phone then took a picture, "If you're lying to me, you'll be killed."

From over his head Lars placed a blow into the Russian's groin, causing one of his testicles to burst. Petrikov passed out with the pain.

Lars searched the Russian's room and found the usual trappings of someone on the run, or maybe a thief like he thought. He mulled over the information he had gained. Maybe the story the Russian had told him was true. Dare he leave him? *No!*

He filled a glass of water from the bathroom and threw it in Petrikov's face, who then slowly opened his eyes.

Lars grabbed him by the throat, "Tell me what you know Russian bastard! It's your last chance."

Through a mouth of blood and a lack of air he mumbled, "Gorod Mertvykh."

Lars repeated the words in Swedish, "De dödas stad!"

Petrikov passed out, Lars shook him to wake him up.

"So, it's true that you were there…Who travelled with you? Who were you with? Give me a name…Talk man… Talk!"

Petrikov managed to spurt out, "My brother," then passed out again.

Lars shook the Russian repeatedly trying to spark some life into the limp body. Unable to wake him, he threw another glass of water into his face but there was no response. He checked for a pulse on the Russians wrist. *Nothing, Skit.*

Lars quickly gathered up the man's belongings and cleaned the room for any traces of himself. From his left pocket he carefully removed the tissue he'd found in Matis's car and dropped it near the waste bin.

He put the "DO NOT DISTURB" sign on the door and slammed the door behind him. Ensuring that his head was down and concealed from the security cameras he left the hotel. After a short walk to confirm that no one was following him he hailed a cab to take him to the airport. The journey out of the city was more enjoyable than the way in.

Seeing the grin on his face the taxi driver asked, "Did you have a good time in our city?"

Lars spat out a reply in Swedish, "Dra åt helvete."

The taxi driver responded in Finnish.

At Helsinki airport Lars called Bergqvist on his mobile.

She answered, "Lars! Tell me the good news."

"Unfortunately, the man died during interrogation, but I got enough information to confirm that he was one of the people from Russia. He first said he found the goods but after some persuasion he mentioned 'Gorod mertvykh'. You know what that means?"

"Of course! I'm not an idiot, de dödas stad, the city of the dead."

"He said that his brother was with him."

"And you believed him? If they were just bank thieves then why was his brother searching my offices and apartment? Lars you disappointed me! You must find this brother or whoever he was. We need to know the true story of why they visited Yacheyka. I don't want any disruption to our plans."

"I took his documents and phone. He said his name was 'Alexandri Sudov', the passport confirms that's his name. I'll get our best people onto tracing his family."

Bergqvist slammed the phone down.

❖ ❖ ❖ ❖

Hilla watched from the roadside as Lars left the hotel. She crossed the road and entered the lobby. She waved to the receptionist and headed to Petrikov's room. She used the spare key to let herself into the room, finding the Russian taking his final breaths. She quickly pulled him down onto the floor and started CPR. In desperation she began beating the Russians chest, tears filled her eyes.

Petrikov suddenly took one large gulp of air and opened his eyes. He began coughing, spitting out blood from his mouth and lungs. Hilla moved him on to his side and he began taking deeper, regular breaths. Hilla moved to the phone to call for an ambulance. Petrikov waved her away from the phone and pointed to the vodka. She passed him the bottle and he gulped down the last dregs before passing out.

❖ ❖ ❖ ❖

Matis returned to the jewellery shop and handed over the rucksack to the owner, "We've made a good return tonight my friend. Quickly turn these into untraceable gems and gold rings. I will return in a few days to collect them. Our contacts in Sweden will be happy to take them off our hands."

Chapter 12
Sterling Lines

Finn joined Mac, Adams, and the MI6 intelligence officers in the base briefing room. He sat and pushed his iBOW across the table to one of the officers, "There are lots of photos on there…see if there's anything useful."

The officer plugged the device into his laptop, downloaded the data onto his screen, studied the images then excitedly said, "I don't believe it."

"What have you found?" Mac asked.

"This image has all the security details for the Existence server." Mac and Finn standing behind the officer watched the laptop screen as he spoke, "These numbers are the IP addresses for the hard drives. They've even given us the encryption key for the security system. It's a classic IT fail, make the computer system secure to deter hackers then write the password and access details on a bit of paper and leave it lying around."

"How does that help us?" Mac enquired.

"It means that along with the trojan horse virus on the USB stick we have everything we need. We can log into their computer server remotely from here and search through all the business documents and emails. If the virus spreads through the network it'll give us access to individual employee laptops and PC's. It's a game changer, we will be able to mine lots of intel, maybe even find some that you can use to find Bergqvist."

"What are you waiting for?"

"I don't have authorisation, it's illegal, we're supposed to get a court order otherwise the evidence is ignored."

"Never mind that crap we might all be dead soon if that weapon is released. Just get on with it, I'll worry about what's illegal or not," Mac barked.

The intelligence officer put his head down and began typing, "No problem. It'll take me awhile to get inside and have a good look around. You're best taking a break, give me thirty minutes."

Mac turned to Finn, "Do you fancy grabbing some food? We'll bring some back for these guys."

"Sounds good…follow me."

The two men made their way to the mess hall and filled their plates from the buffet, picked up a couple of drinks and found an empty table. They ate shepherd's pie with peas, carrots, and roast potatoes.

Finn returned for a second helping. Mac sat in silence and studied the SAS soldier in front of him as he ate his food plate. He considered the details that the reports had contained. In this setting he appeared to be nothing like the ruthless killing machine that Adams had told him about. The reports of what Finn had done in the field had left him in no doubt.

Finn pushed his empty plate away, leaned back in the chair and asked, "What's your story then? You told me in Finland that you're not 'a suit'. You may have changed your clothes but I'm still dubious about trusting you."

"Thanks for the vote of confidence. My story is just like yours really. I joined the Royal Marines and served with them for nine years. Got into a few scrapes around the world, got a few promotions, one of those was to Military Intelligence. The naturally progression was to a senior position at MI6. It's different from army life but I enjoy it, especially when we catch the bad guys."

Finn said with a grin, "So you're telling me that you used to be a Bootneck, who'd have believed it? I take back my comments…maybe you're not 'a suit' after all."

"I'm not sure how to take that but believe me I was tempted to come to Russia with you but using Petrikov was the preferential option. How did you get on with him?"

"All I'll say is that he's certainly a character. He did what he promised and got me in and out safely, can't say more than that. Come on…we should get back to the briefing room."

The two men collected food and drinks for the four intelligence officers and returned to the briefing room. Finn told Mac to forget Adams, "He can get his own."

The intelligence officers took a break and ate their meals while Finn and Mac looked through the latest intel documents.

The intelligence officer who accessed the Existence server put his empty plate on the table and sat at his laptop, "I'm still going through the bulk of the files but I've got some information that will get you started."

Mac and Finn joined him and Mac said, "Fire away, we're listening."

"I've not found anything yet which indicates that they're planning anything. I've searched for multiple keywords and it's blank. They may have another server or system somewhere that has that stuff on it. This server is just a front for the legitimate side of the business. It shows that the company accounts have a healthy balance sheet and they've been using spare cash to buy up large areas of land in the north. They also bought a disused mine from Urmina, the father's mining business. They're calling the place Början, that's Swedish for 'beginning'. I looked it up on Google translate. The invoices rolling through the accounts system indicate that they've invested lots of money in the place. I've found lots of invoices for construction work and equipment."

"Where's this Början place?" Mac asked.

"In the north, near Kiruna."

"Anything else?"

"I managed to trace the second man killed at Yacheyka, Patrik Lind. His file says he was thirty-three and employed as a security expert. Along with the other guy, Wallin, he pays taxes and seems legit."

"So, he looks like a dead-end," Mac said, the disappointment evident in his voice.

"Not quite, I searched the Interpol database and he was arrested in Ibiza along with Bergqvist during the drug bust. Seems like the father got a top lawyer involved and did a deal for a suspended sentence for him as well. Bergqvist, Lind and Wallin all went to university together. With more digging online I found a newspaper article with a picture showing the three of them, plus another guy called Lars, at an environmental protest in Germany. It appears the four of them are close, all have strong ties to the environmentalist groups around the world."

"A group of university eco-warriors taking eco ideas to an extreme level," Finn quipped.

"Good work! We need to trace this Lars person. If he's still part of the group then he's most likely involved somewhere and might lead us to the weapon." Mac urged.

"What about the picture above the bed? It seemed important. Have you traced anything from the label on the back?" Finn asked.

The intelligence officer on their right spoke up from behind his computer screen, "Akkajaure Lake is a place up in the north of the country. There's a hydroelectric plant there. The land all around is owned by Existence."

"Does the home in the picture exist?"

"Give me a moment…" The intelligence officer opened the internet browser on his laptop and opened Google maps. A quick search for Akkajaure brought up a satellite image of the lake. With Finn's original image open on another screen as a reference, he began zooming in and moving along the banks of the lake until he stopped and pointed at the screen, "That's got to be it."

"Get the coordinates, that's my new lead," Finn announced.

"What are you thinking?" Mac asked.

"You need to find out what you can about this Lars person. I'm no-good sitting around on my arse, I need to be in the field. That house on the lake means something, I need to check it out, it might be where she's holed up, if not it might yield some more intel for us."

"Sounds like a plan," Mac agreed.

"All the evidence that we're gathering points to the Lapland area of Sweden." Finn moved to a map on the wall and pointed while speaking, "This is Lapland, there's Kiruna, the mine is nearby. There's Lake Akkajaure where the house is. There can't be more than a hundred miles maximum between the two places. We need to relocate nearby. We're wasting time with all this travelling."

Mac looked at Adams, "It makes sense, what do you think?"

Adams shrugged his shoulders, Mac made the decision for him, "Okay guys start packing all this gear up. I'll speak to my guys at MI6 and arrange for a safe house somewhere in that area to use as a new base of operations."

Adams opened his mouth to protest. Mac recognised the look and added, "Don't worry you can stay here and offer support if it's needed."

Finn noted the look of relief on Adam's face and felt happy that his CO was staying behind, one less person for him to look after.

Mac contacted his office and after a series of calls finally managed to speak to an MI6 agent working in Sweden. He organised a safe house near Gällivare Airport, a small municipal airport in Lapland between Kiruna and Akkajaure. After putting the phone down, he announced, "We're leaving."

Chapter 13
Början

Lars arrived at the converted mine as the evening sun began to settle on the horizon. The cool summer breeze blew dust off the scattered mounds of mine tailings causing a haze in the red sky.

Once clear of security and the decontamination process, he walked to tunnel four, into the accommodation sector and on to his private room. After stowing his gear, he headed to tunnel five and the IT sector, finding the room stocked with the latest computer and digital storage equipment. Internet access was possible via a satellite uplink provided by a Chinese company, routed into multiple VPN access points. Nils had designed the system to ensure government agencies could not trace digital traffic back to the facility.

Lars was surprised to find only one person working in a small office, a young woman, "Where are all the staff? We've got lots of work to complete if we're to be ready in the next few days."

The woman replied nervously, "The others have finished for the evening but the computers are doing all the real work. I'm the night shift operator here for computer maintenance and data archiving."

"Do your computer skills include tracing a person for me?"

"I can try, give me the details."

"I need you to find a man called Alexandri Sudov, a Russian, around forty years of age. I met him at the Regent Hotel in Helsinki two days ago and before that he was in Russia. Unfortunately, someone mugged him at the hotel and died. I need to find his next of kin and send our condolences. Check all the airports and ferry terminals to find out when and where he entered the country. He may have travelled from Russia or via somewhere else in Europe. See what you can find on him, family, friends, work, everything."

Lars left the computer operator to the task and moved to tunnel seven and the research sector, finding Molantra and another scientist working in different areas of the laboratory. Annoyed that they did not acknowledge his arrival he shouted, "Molantra!"

The Indian engineer turned to face the Swede with a blank expression, not displaying the real anger he felt inside.

"How far have you got with creating the device?" Lars barked.

"It's nearly ready. Come with me and I'll show you what we've done," the Indian engineer gestured for him to follow to an area at the back of the laboratory. "This is what we've come up with. As you instructed, I've designed the unit to be portable with remote operation. To create the device quickly we've used standard parts that are readily available on the market. This is the best solution with the timescales you've given me."

Lars studied the device. Four nineteen-kilogram gas cylinders strapped together in a square configuration, on top a black box with wires and a digital display. The device was compact and portable and less than one metre in length.

Lars smiled, "This is perfect, exactly as I imagined. What's the overall weight and fluid volume?"

"The weight will be around ninety kilograms. The total volume of the gas bottles is eight cubic metres."

"Good. Explain how it works."

"The gas bottles hold the solution under pressure. I've created two ways to activate the device, by a timer or by remote trigger. The electronics control the valves on the gas bottles. Once activated the valves will open and distribute the contents into the atmosphere as a fine mist. If using the timer, you can override it remotely."

"What's the maximum range of the remote switch?"

"The device and the remote switch use the same electronic circuits as a standard mobile telephone however the data stream encryption key is programmed into the device and remote trigger. Only the two matching parts can activate the device. By using satellite communication, you could be in another country if you wish. However, it'll only work if both the user and the device have line of sight to the satellite."

"And what's the area that will be covered by the mist once the device is activated?"

"It depends on the height of the device and the wind conditions. How do you intend to use it? Will it be fitted to a plane or used at ground level on a vehicle?" Molantra enquired.

"We intend to install the device on the roof of a building. In that scenario what area would the mist cover?"

"If it's installed at a height of five to ten stories and used on a day with a mild breeze it should cover a radius of ten to twenty miles."

"This will work perfectly. When can it be ready?"

"We need to know more about the biological substance. We must calculate the dilution ratio of the solution to achieve distribution over a large area. To create the delivery system and determine the gas nozzle size, we need to know the final viscosity and we cannot create the solution without the sample. When will you provide it? You keep ordering us to work faster whilst holding us back."

"You'll get it soon, continue with your work, get everything ready so the device can be finalised once it's here."

"What's this biological substance that you've created? What's it for? The project was to create a delivery system for a new type of pesticide, that's what the agent in Dubai said. It was made clear that it was for agricultural purposes only, now you're saying that it'll be installed on a building."

"None of your business! I ask the questions, don't get ahead of yourself Molantra."

The Indian engineer moved uneasily, "Is this a weapon of some kind? Who are you people?"

Lars struck the engineer across the face with the back of his hand, causing him to fall to the floor. Standing over him he shouted, "Shut up! You ask too many questions. It's bad for your health, now get on with your work."

Lars took a final look at the device then exited the laboratory.

Molantra struggled to his feet and walked over to the other scientist, a chemist, "I have a bad feeling about this, we don't know what this substance is or why they want to disperse it into the atmosphere. Why all the secrecy?"

The chemist replied in a voice no louder than a whisper, "Be careful they're listening, the room has cameras and listening devices. I'm also worried about what they're planning to do. This isn't what I signed up for. I thought I would be working for an environmental company that wanted to develop new substances to replace conventional fertilisers. Since I've been here, they've never wanted to discuss any of my ideas on the subject. I've asked to leave many times and every time I'm told, 'Not until the work is complete'. I don't trust them."

"It appears that they lured us both here on false promises. My work for the Indian government on the creation of lightweight crop-dusting equipment was their only interest. I was promised over one hundred thousand euros to complete their project in a quick time."

A security guard walked into the laboratory during his rounds and the two scientists quickly moved apart and continued working.

❖ ❖ ❖ ❖

Lars sat up on the bed in his room, called Bergqvist and received a curt response, "Lars!"

"Good evening! I'm back from Helsinki. I've got our computer team tracing the Russian thief, hopefully they'll turn up something which tells us why they visited Yacheyka."

"That's why you called me? I don't need to micromanage you…do I? Just call when you've got some information that I can use."

Lars paused, his instinct told him to curse and disconnect the call instead he held his words.

"Lars? Are you still there?"

"Yes, you did not allow me to finish. The reason I called was to tell you that the device is ready. The engineer needs the biological substance to proceed. When will you come here?"

"That's good news, things are progressing. I'll come tomorrow sometime, most likely in the evening."

"Agneta, you sound angry, or frustrated, which is it?"

"I guess it's frustration. We're so close to our dream and yet the incident at the offices is playing on my mind."

"Don't worry about that, I'm dealing with it. One of the thieves is dead, we're tracing the other one. Once I find him, I can assure you that he'll meet the same fate."

"Let's change the subject, tell me more about the device."

"It's portable, around eighty kilos, operated by satellite phone and will spread particles over a ten-to-twenty-mile radius."

"That's great," Bergqvist said excitedly.

"Have you thought of a target?"

"I've chosen Ghaziabad, India. The inhabitants have the record for producing the highest level of pollution in the last year. Let's start there."

"I've never heard of it."

"It's in the north of the country with a population of around one point seven million. They call it the gateway to the Uttar Pradesh region. High volumes of cars, trucks, motorbikes, tuk tuks, and buses all making their way in and out of the city, releasing large volumes of pollution. The local officials refuse to do anything about the vehicles and industry destroying the air quality. The animals and plants are dying all around the city, we'll just finish the job for them and get rid of the cause at the same time."

"The cause?"

"The humans!"

Lars imagined masses of dead bodies lying in the streets. Bergqvist imagined the resulting tranquil setting as the planet gradually returned to life.

Bergqvist broke the silence, "Have you finalised the plan on how you will deploy the device?"

"Mostly, however I need to research the location. The scientist said that if we position the device at a high level it'll ensure maximum coverage, a five to ten storey building should do. More importantly, we need to consider the organisational challenges of transporting the device and installing it without detection."

"It sounds like you'll have another late night. When I arrive make sure you've got all of the answers to those questions."

The line went dead.

Lars dreamed of their younger happier days when they loved each other. The days before her hatred of her father consumed her life. Twisting hatred into a cause. A cause to die for.

Chapter 14
Gällivare, Lapland

Finn, Mac, and the intelligence officers continued standing outside the small terminal building at Gällivare Airport and wondered why the arranged transport was late. The unmarked executive jet they'd used was on its way back to the UK within minutes of landing. The cool northern air and a light mist greeted them. The customs paperwork, supplied by Mac, detailed the crates containing electronic, military, and personal gear as equipment for geological research. The officer quickly looked and stamped the documents, showing no interest as he passed them back.

A Ford Transit crew bus drove into the carpark and screeched to a halt. Out of the driver's side climbed a large man. Finn estimated that he was six foot three tall and over three hundred pounds in weight. Not the sort of person you want falling on you in a fight.

The man approached the group and singled out Mac, "I'm Strom. You're the MI6 man?"

"Yes…"

Strom cut Mac off from adding anymore, "I don't need to know your names, I got the usual intel files with your pictures. It's best that way. Just get your gear loaded, we need to get out of here before the locals start asking questions."

The men loaded the gear into the Transit and climbed inside. Strom floored the accelerator and they began the journey to the safe house. The old diesel transit rattled and strained to get up to speed on the winding country roads.

On the way Strom shouted out above the noise, "I've got a cabin about ten miles from the airport. It's network secure with a satellite uplink. Out here in the wilderness there are lots of remote cabins and lodges. We'll not raise any suspicion if people act normally. The customs guys at the airport are on the payroll, hence why you just walked through. The locals are not on the payroll so don't do things that will raise their suspicions like causing trouble. Just be nice and polite."

"What do you know about why we're here?" Mac asked.

"Nothing. I keep this place open for various agencies, mainly those affiliated with NATO. That doesn't include us Swedes, we don't like NATO. The location makes it a convenient drop off point for agents passing through Russia and beyond. It's used for covert operations and to hide assets when required. My job is just to keep the safe house active and ready to accept guests. You're safe to do whatever it is that you're doing."

Strom pulled the Transit off the main road and onto an unpaved farm track that led down to a two-storey wooden clad building. The dull yellow painted building was dilapidated with flaky paint and a steel sheeted roof. Finn imagined the noise that the roof would create when it rained. To one side of the building there was a separate garage big enough for three to four vehicles.

The Transit pulled to a stop and the men began unloading the gear. They moved everything into the hallway of the property and Strom took them on a quick guided tour. He showed them the living quarters, kitchen, bathroom, bedrooms.

Finn noted the shabby decor, broken furniture and the smell of rot and mould in the old wooden walls and floors. It reminded him of the barracks room in Afghanistan where the rancid air of flatulence regularly greeted him.

On the upper landing Strom smiled, "You can fight between yourselves for the bedrooms, but stay out of mine."

Finn made a mental point of making sure to stay out of Strom's bedroom then followed the big man downstairs to the lower floor.

Strom said excitedly, "Now for the fun stuff."

He led them down a set of stairs to the basement where they found a room different to the structure above. Modern walls, floors, electrics, heating, and lighting. In the middle of the room there was a series of desks with computers and other electronics equipment. Along one wall there was a bank of televisions showing various data streams. Finn noted the look of pleasure on the intelligence officer's faces.

"You guys can get set up here, I want you to keep searching that server for intel," Mac instructed.

Strom gestured to Finn and Mac to follow him to a room at the back of the basement. He punched in a code on a keypad and stepped back as the doors opened. Finn and

Mac studied the contents, racks containing weapons, uniforms and the latest military and covert surveillance equipment filled the walls.

Finn walked in and picked up an assault rifle from a gun rack, a Heckler & Koch HK416. He checked the magazine was empty then played with the red eye scope and listened to the trigger mechanism. He put the rifle down and reached onto a shelf and picked out a SIG Sauer P320 semi-automatic pistol, "Do you have silencers for these?"

"Of course," Strom confirmed, then turned to Mac and asked, "Do you want to have a play?"

"No, that stuff is more his thing," Mac said dryly.

"When you're finished let's go up to the garage," Strom suggested.

"We can go now. I've seen what I need," Finn replied.

Strom led them to a side door in the basement and down a corridor to another staircase leading upwards. Strom disappeared up the stairs with Mac and Finn close behind.

When Finn arrived at the top, he walked out into another heavily modified interior, nothing like the dilapidated garage facade outside. High density wood chip insulated walls, modern flooring, high power lighting, halogen heating and racks of tools made the garage a piston head's dream.

Parked inside was a black heavily modified Toyota Landcruiser with raised suspension and wide all terrain wheels. Four Polaris snowmobiles sat on a rack mounted along the back wall with a lift system. On a trailer beside the Landcruiser was a four-seater Air Rider Hovercraft with the latest navigation system. Finally, they noticed two Yamaha YZ450 dirt bikes on a trailer, occupying the last parking bay.

"Everything that you need to get around out here. It may be sunny and dry now but the weather can change quickly and the winters are extreme. If you want to take anything the keys are over there on the rack, just remember to replace them when you're finished. That completes the tour, you've got work to do and I'm starving." Strom patted his belly then disappeared down the stairs.

"What do you think?" Mac asked.

"We've got everything we need to take things to the next level that's for sure. Let's face it Mac, things are going to get messy if we're going to get that weapon back safely. I'm going to the lakeside house to see what's there. You stay here and see what's on the Existence computers."

"What if you get there and find she has an army of guards? You've got no support," Mac said, concerned for the man who he now considered a friend.

"I don't intend to take anyone on in battle, it's a recon mission. I'm going to get intel only, in and out without detection. All the equipment I need is here so we may as well use it."

Finn and Mac returned to the comms room, joining the intelligence officers who had completed setting up their gear.

Mac gently banged his fist on the table, "Right everyone let's all stay focused, we still have a job to do. We need an action plan…what have we got so far that we can use?"

Finn returned to the weapons store and started selecting the gear he would need. He reviewed the selection of uniforms on the rack and started looking through the ones with splinter camouflage for his size. He had encountered the Swedish army uniform before, specially designed for use in the forests and plains of the country. He quickly changed his clothes, including putting on a set of matching Swedish army boots. Finally, he stuck a union jack badge on the Velcro arm patch and replaced the cover flap. Once dressed and ready, Finn chose his weapons and some extras and placed them into a black holdall.

He walked out of the weapons store into the main Comms room and said to Mac, "I'm off now! You can follow my progress by tracking the iBOW, and message me if find any intel on Lars. I'll give you an update when I arrive at the house."

"No problem…good luck, and remember…no rough stuff, if it gets nasty get the hell out of there and I'll arrange some backup."

Finn waved the concerns away and returned upstairs to the house. In the kitchen he made up a pack with food and water then left the house. He crossed over the yard to the garage and loaded the gear into the back of the Toyota Landcruiser. He pulled the big four-by-four out of the garage so he could hook up the trailer for the hovercraft. He opened the GPS application on the iBOW and entered the coordinates for the lakeside house.

Chapter 15
Helsinki

Petrikov woke up on the hotel bed and looked around the room. Blood covered the floor and the bed sheets. He rubbed his face with his hand, the pain from the broken nose made him flinch. He placed his two hands in a praying position, grabbed his nose and quickly reset the bone. He let out a groan and tasted the blood on his lips. He ran his tongue around his mouth and felt the gaps in his teeth. He took a moment to recollect the events that had taken place, taking a mental picture of his assailants, the blonde-haired Swede who had tried to kill him, the large bodyguard who had caught him off guard and the other man, the one who laughed while the Swede beat him. He remembered him taking the jewels and his dream of a new life. He cursed the thief and vowed revenge.

He sat up on the bed and cursed his luck. He stood and staggered to the toilet, the pain searing in his balls as he walked. He relieved himself and watched as the thick yellow and blood-tinged water splashed against the white porcelain bowl. Once finished he dropped his pants and looked at his genitals, his ball sack swollen, black and blue. The deep yellow, red, and purple bruise had already begun to spread onto his inner thighs and down his legs. He cursed the Swede who had destroyed his sex life and vowed revenge.

He looked in the mirror and gazed at the gaps in his teeth. He thought of the bodyguard and vowed revenge.

To relieve the pain that he felt on every part of his body he took a long hot bath. While he laid in the soapy water, he drew up his plan. He thought of Hilla, the young woman who had followed him to the bar. How he had watched as she stood in the rain waiting for him. It did not take long for him to convince her to join him. She told the story of the old shop owner who groped her at every chance and how she wished she change her life. The offer of riches beyond her dreams made it easy to convert her to his way of thinking. Along with the money that he had promised he also now owed her his life. For her sake he had to get the stolen money back.

He dressed, taking care not to touch his groin, and ordered room service, including a fresh bottle of vodka. Once fed and watered he considered his options, without a passport and money, they were currently limited. He used the room telephone to call the local office and arranged for an agent to leave a new passport, money, and a weapon at the train station drop box. The office also arranged for a local doctor, sympathetic to the cause, to make a room call. A doctor who would not ask questions. After a quick check-up the doctor gave him the drugs that would gradually heal him and keep the pain away while the process happened.

He laid on the bed, closed his eyes and thought of his plan. A gentle tapping on the hotel room door interrupted the silence. Taking much greater care than he did before he fitted the security chain and slowly opened the door. The young woman stood nervously on the other side. Quickly removing the chain, he invited her in, "Hilla, I'm glad to see you,"

Hilla walked inside nervously, "I don't have much time. I came for the money you promised?"

Petrikov rubbed his head and sat on the edge of the bed, "There's the problem. Your boss has taken the money. I need your help to get it back."

"My boss? No…he's not the one who came here, that was Matis. But my boss has your jewellery. I noticed it at the store today, he's going to break it down so he can sell it on. He's agreed to split the money with Matis."

"Not if I take it back first and to do that, I need your help. If you help me, I'll give you double the amount I originally promised," Petrikov urged.

Hilla hesitated, frightened for her life, trapped in a bad situation, wishing she had not accepted the Russian's offer of a drink, "How can I help you? I don't know how to get your money back."

"Leave that to me. Tell me about the Swede, who was he?"

"I don't know, it was arranged by Matis."

"Ok, I'll ask him when I see him later."

Petrikov discussed his plan. Hilla left the hotel and returned twenty minutes later with two cheap mobile phones. Petrikov opened the boxes and set up the phones, storing the numbers in each phone. He passed one to Hilla, "Don't lose this, it has my number, I've got yours."

Together they walked to the train station.

Petrikov collected the items from the drop box, safely storing the passport and money in his inside jacket pockets. He picked up the paper bag with the gun and wrapped it in a newspaper then headed towards the station toilets with Hilla following close behind, "Wait outside, I'll only be a few moments."

Inside the toilets he moved to the urinal, the newspaper tucked under his armpit. He pretended to urinate while waiting for an old man two urinals down to finish his business. He shook his head in disgust as the man walked out without washing his hands. He checked to make sure the cubicles were empty and chose the last one. He took out the gun, a GSh-18PT pistol with a full eighteen bullet magazine and in the bottom of the bag he found a silencer and an extra magazine. He fitted the silencer, tucked the pistol into the back of his trousers and stashed the extra magazine in a pocket. Before exiting the toilet, he checked to make sure the back of his jacket was down and covering the pistol.

Back in the station concourse he approached Hilla and declared, "Okay, I'm ready. Let's go and get my money."

After a short walk they arrived at the jewellery store and watched from over the road as the owner served a customer. Once the customer left he told Hilla to wait, then casually walked over the road and into the store. As he entered the owner immediately recognised his face and reached for the panic button.

Petrikov quickly pulled out the pistol and shouted, "Leave it." He mentally thanked Hilla for the information.

The owner stepped back and raised his hands. Petrikov noticed the petrified look on the man's face, "Move, come out from there, lock the door, the shop is closed for business."

The owner followed the instructions with Petrikov guarding his every move. Once complete, Petrikov led him back behind the counter and into the small room. He pushed the man down into a chair and pointed the pistol at his head, "Where's the bag of jewellery and money?"

"I don't have it," the owner mumbled.

Petrikov felt a twinge of pain in his balls, the drugs beginning to wear off, his patience began to wear thin, "Once again! Where's the bag?"

"Please, I don't have it."

Petrikov shot the man's shoulder, tearing through the flesh and shattering the bone, "That's the wrong answer. I've got seventeen more bullets that I can use to make this a very painful experience for you."

The man cried in pain and muttered, "The safe, it's in the safe."

"Open it!"

The man struggled to his feet and moved a wall panel to reveal a large safe. Fighting the pain, he managed to enter the code and open the door ajar before staggering to the chair. Petrikov swung the door open and looked inside finding jewellery trays, bundles of cash and on the top shelf his rucksack. He pulled it out, placed it on the table and checked the contents. He reached inside the safe and took some diamond rings and a bundle of cash adding that to his original stash, "That's payment for the beating your friend gave me, do you agree?"

Between sobs of pain the jeweller nodded.

"Good, now call this man Matis, make him come here. Tell him you've been robbed or something, anything, just make sure you get him to come here."

The man composed himself, stood up and called, using a phone on the wall, "Matis we've got a problem, the police came here asking about the stolen jewels. You need to come straight away and take them."

A few moments of silence followed before the man replaced the handset, "He's on his way."

"Good!" Petrikov lifted the gun and shot the man in the forehead. The bullet exited the back of his skull, spraying most of the man's brain onto the wall.

The Russian moved to the front of the shop. He hid behind the display window, looking out into the street. He watched as several customers tried the door then walked away disappointed. An old black car pulled up outside and he watched as the bodyguard got out and opened the passenger door. Out stepped the other man from the hotel. *Matis!*

As the two men approached, Petrikov unlocked the shop door and hid from view. The door swung open and the bodyguard entered with Matis following. Once far enough inside the shop Petrikov slammed the door behind them and flicked the lock. The two men turned, startled to see the Russian behind them holding a gun.

"Welcome comrades!" Petrikov declared. "I'm ready for you this time, no chance for a sucker punch." He gestured with the pistol, "Move, get in the backroom."

As they entered the backroom, they discovered the dead body of the owner, slumped in the chair. Matis panicked and nervously announced, "My friend, we can sort this misunderstanding out between us. You can take the jewellery, I have more if you want it."

Petrikov ignored the comments and shoved Matis into the back of the bodyguard and the two men stumbled into the room. The bodyguard pulled a pistol from his jacket and turned. Petrikov was quicker. The bullet entered the bodyguard's neck, tearing his carotid artery in half and spraying blood over Matis's face and coat. As the bodyguard fell to the ground with blood quickly draining from his brain, his finger squeezed the trigger on the pistol. The bullet skimmed along the floor and amputated two toes from Matis's left foot.

Matis screamed in pain and collapsed, landing on top of the bodyguard's dead body.

Petrikov laughed loudly, "Oh Shut up! Stop acting like a baby."

"Please comrade, don't kill me. I've got money, lots of money, I'll give it all to you."

"I don't want your money. You're a parasite, an embarrassment to the great nation of Russia. You've used your power and contacts to feed off other people for too many years, sucking the life out of good people, good Russians. Times are changing in the motherland my old friend. You only have yourself to blame, you chose to ignore the warnings about your black-market dealings. Instead, you chose to move to Finland and continue with your dirty deeds here. Things have finally caught up with you."

"If you kill me then you'll only be killing yourself, I've got connections in the Party."

"Your connections to the Party have been terminated. Now stop your whining and tell me about the Swede."

"The Swede?"

"The man you brought to my hotel room. Start talking and I'll make it quick."

"I got his details from a black-market dealer in Sweden. All I know is that he works for a company called Existence. I don't know any more than that. Please comrade, let me go."

"Where are the contact details for this Swede?"

"In my phone," Matis fumbled in his pocket and took out his mobile. "Look for 'Lars', that's his name."

Petrikov snatched the phone and snarled, "The passcode!"

"120262."

Petrikov used the code to unlock the phone then scrolled through the contacts until he found what he needed, "Thank you…Comrade!" He shot Matis in the head, killing him instantly. He went through the safe and took two more bundles of cash and jewellery and stuffed them in his trouser pocket whilst putting the rucksack on. At the front door he engaged the lock mechanism ensuring the door locked as he exited.

Walking over the road to Hilla he pulled out the jewels and cash and announced, "Here. You don't need to worry about those men anymore. I suggest you leave the country, start a new life somewhere."

Hilla accepted the items and stared at them for several moments. She was about to reply when she noticed the Russian getting into a large black SUV. Petrikov looked at the young woman through the passenger side window, smiled then gave a signal to the driver to set off. His thoughts turned to the task of tracing the Swede.

Chapter 16
Akkajaure Lake

Finn sat in the Toyota Landcruiser and reviewed the suggested route offered by the GPS, one hundred and fifteen miles by road with another ten on top by foot. He smiled to himself knowing that he would be taking a direct route that would reduce the distance by at least forty miles. The route to the entrance of the Stubba Nature Reserve was his priority, then he would make his own choices.

He started the diesel engine and set off down the farm track and onto the main single lane road. Now heading West with the sun reflecting off the road he put on his sunglasses and enjoyed the drive. The first part of the journey was uneventful apart from the angry local who overtook him at speed blasting the horn as he passed. Finn assumed that in such a remote location the locals did not always follow the speed limits. Unfortunately, speeding was a luxury he could not afford. The risk of an over diligent traffic officer stopping him, then discovering a cache of weapons in the boot, was something to avoid.

He pulled off the main road into an empty unpaved carpark at the start of the Stubba Nature Reserve, a vast expanse of land covered in forests, barren land, mountain ranges and lakes. He moved the Landcruiser up to a metal gate with a warning sign in Swedish. Finn smashed the padlock with a rock, opened the gate and quickly pulled the jeep and trailer inside. After closing the gate, he refitted the broken padlock to provide a visual deterrent if someone was following him. He climbed into the jeep and looked along the dirt track as it headed through the sparsely populated forest into the distance.

The track was easy going for the modified Landcruiser, the large wheels and raised suspension perfect for the uneven terrain. The supercharged diesel engine barely ticked over as he maintained a safe speed. The track weaved through the forest and with each mile the trees became fewer and further apart. Every mile or so he encountered a fork in the track which made him stop. On most occasions he could decide the correct route by the orientation of the sun, on others he consulted the map displayed on the GPS application.

He continued to follow the track into a valley between two mountain ranges. At the end of the valley the land flattened out, the trees disappeared, leaving a barren landscape with scattered ponds and mini lakes. The track split into a 'Y' shape, both routes seeming to head in the direction he needed to go. He consulted the GPS map and discovered that Satihaure Lake, his destination, was now very close.

The ground became wetter. He engaged low gear and the large all terrain tyres made easy work of the mud. He drove on the muddy and heavily rutted track for a few more miles, the elevation dropping as he proceeded, indicating that he was heading down towards water level. A few miles further, at a bend in the track, he came over the crest of a hill and surveyed the large expanse of water that spread out in front of him.

Finn moved the Landcruiser down to the water's edge and turned the vehicle around to aim the trailer at the water. He unloaded the items he required from the boot before locking the jeep and stowing the keys in a pocket.

He transferred the rucksack, assault rifle and night vision goggles to the hovercraft. The task of turning the handle on the tilting mechanism was difficult at first, the newness of the paint still on the threads. Eventually the back of the trailer touched the sand on the lake shore and he began unclipping the security straps holding the craft in place.

With only the front strap preventing the craft to slide off the trailer, Finn quickly climbed onboard. He started the engine and let the propeller rotate at idle speed while the belt driven air pump inflated the large rubber skirt. The hovercraft fidgeted from side to side on the trailer bed from gravity and the propeller motion. Finally, he took the driver's seat and flipped the lock mechanism holding the front strap.

The hovercraft began sliding backwards off the trailer and down to the water's edge. Finn increased the revs on the engine and pulled the steering stick to the left, turning the craft around one hundred and eighty degrees. With the water now in front of him he pushed the accelerator lever further forward. The propeller speed increased slightly, pushing the craft out into the deeper water of the lake. With the hovercraft half afloat, half hovering, Finn entered the coordinates for the house into the screen on the built-in Sat Nav. Once the direct, and impossible A to B route appeared he zoomed in on the map and set the required waypoints. The first few waypoints to ensure he stayed on a safe course in the centre of the lake and the latter ones to chart the course to Akkajaure Lake.

The low sun began to set behind a mountain, turning the waveless lake a dull black and grey. He pushed the throttle forward, adjusting the propeller speed to a comfortable level. The hovercraft skimmed along the top of the water and headed towards the far end of the lake.

After a journey of fifteen miles the Sat Nav beeped to warn him that the small tributary to Akkajaure Lake was nearby. The light faded as he approached the mountain that divided the two lakes. He slowed the engine, reducing both speed and noise, and put on his night vision goggles. The landscape in front of him turned black with distinctive green coloured shades and lines highlighting the way.

The hovercraft entered the tributary, a link that nature had carved out of the mountain joining the two lakes and a means for water to drain away when the winter levels became too high. Currently, in the summer season the tributary was mostly dry, with only the deepest parts still containing some water. The dense forest that covered the mountain on both sides offered additional protection and reduced the risk of detection.

Finn praised himself for his earlier research of the area but it did not mean it was going to be easy. The first obstacle was the low bridge that joined the forest track running along the shore of the lake. Finn pushed the throttle forward and drove the hovercraft up the embankment and onto the dirt track. Not wanting to hang around he continued down the other side and splashed into the water. He slowed the engine to a crawl and weaved along the sections of dry riverbed and ponds. The Sat Nav beeped again, warning him of an upcoming settlement, a small group of hunting and fishing cabins used by tourists in the summer. He reduced the propeller speed as low as possible to ensure the craft still moved but with the lowest noise output. He cleared under the second but much higher bridge, and entered Akkajaure Lake.

The midnight sun was now very low on the horizon, giving a strange twilight effect. He stuffed the night vision goggles into the rucksack. The hovercraft bobbed on the gentle waves until he was clear of the settlement, then he increased the speed.

Now on the final leg of the journey, and the most dangerous, his instincts came alive. He scanned the area around him for danger. After travelling another ten miles the Sat Nav indicated that he was within two hundred yards of the house. He stopped the engine and turned sharply to the shore. The residual momentum carried the hovercraft towards the bank until the rubber skirt skidded to a halt on the sand. He jumped off the craft and struggled with the weight as he pulled it further up onto the shore. He found a fallen tree trunk and quickly tied the strap to secure the craft.

Chapter 17
GRU Safehouse, Helsinki

On the outskirts of Helsinki, in a detached property, the Finnish section of GRU First Directorate staff continued with their tasks, a group of seven GRU military intelligence officers assigned to monitor and infiltrate Finnish military and government departments. Section leader, Lieutenant Yelena Roslakova, saluted as Petrikov entered the property. She was surprised to see his face covered in cuts and bruises.

Petrikov dumped his holdall and announced, "Let's not trouble ourselves with such formalities Lieutenant. I'm currently involved in a mission and I need help from your section."

"Of course, Major Petrikov. Headquarters told me to expect you. I've recalled some agents from the field and I've prepared a room for you. Let me show you the way."

"Later! Take me to your team, I need you to hack into a mobile phone." Petrikov growled.

Roslakova showed Petrikov to a ground floor room fitted out with electronic intelligence gathering equipment. The two intelligence officers, a middle-aged man, and a younger woman, working at computers quickly stood and saluted. Petrikov motioned with his hands for them to sit.

Roslakova walked over to the dark-haired woman, "Major this is our best computer expert, Khristina."

Petrikov handed over Matis's phone, "Khristina, I want all of the data off this phone. Especially the contacts and a list of all the calls made in the last few weeks. The passcode is twelve zero two sixty-two. I'm especially interested in the calls that the user has made to people in Sweden. One of the contacts is Lars Wiking. I need to know where that person is now. I'll return within the hour to check on your progress, make sure you've got something for me."

Khristina nodded in acknowledgement. She took the phone and connected it to a laptop and began typing, "Yes Major, I'll do my best."

Petrikov moved to the doorway to leave the room, "Don't disappoint me Khristina, I need you to do better than your best."

In the corridor Petrikov turned to Roslakova, "Show me to my room?"

Roslakova motioned towards the stairs, "This way Major."

Petrikov struggled up the stairs. With each step he took the muscles required to lift his foot pulled at the tender flesh around his groin.

Roslakova noticed the relief on his face when he arrived at the landing, "Major you appear to be in some discomfort. Do you need any medical assistance? We've got a fully stocked medical room downstairs and I'm a trained nurse. Would you like me to give you a check over?"

"Thank you for the offer Lieutenant but I don't think you can help me with my particular problem. Time is the only thing that will heal me. I've already got some painkillers. Do you have any anti-inflammatory gel?"

She pointed to the room at the end of the landing, "This is your room Major please make yourself at home, I'll return with the gel. I would be happy to assist you in any way. I can massage the affected area with the gel if you like."

Petrikov opened the room door and acknowledged the offer of help, "Thank you Lieutenant, I may take you up on the offer."

Inside he undressed, dumped his old clothes in the bin and showered. The hot water eased the pain from the damage on his face and body. He heard a knock at the door and shouted, "Come in."

Roslakova entered the room with the medicine and observed the naked Petrikov through the bathroom door.

"Bring them here," he barked.

She placed the gel tube on the sink and stared at the bruises, cuts and scars all over his body, including a huge bruise around his groin.

"Thank you. Can you take my old clothes, they must be incinerated?"

She grabbed the clothes from the bin and quickly left, relieved that he chose to turn down her offer to administer the gel.

He stopped the shower, grabbed a towel, and gently dried himself. The bruise on his inner thighs was now a mixture of deep purple and yellow. He took the tube from the sink and sat on the toilet seat, allowing his tackle to swing freely. With a large dollop of gel on his fingers he gently massaged the Ibuprofen into his balls, taking care not to hinder the healing process. The cooling gel gave some immediate comfort until he stood up and banged his tackle against the seat. He winced with the intense pain, cursed the Swede, and vowed revenge.

On the sink top he noticed the two pill bottles the doctor had given him. He walked to the sink and stood for a moment looking at his reflection in the mirror. The bruising around his eyes had now turned a deep purple colour. He opened his mouth and used his fingers to see the gaps where his lower left teeth had once been. He reminisced how he'd looked after those teeth through many different assignments, regardless of the situation he always brushed. He narrowed his eyes and cursed the Swede.

He picked up the pill bottles and tipped two painkiller tablets and two anti-inflammatory tablets onto the palm of his hand. He moved to the bedroom, found the vodka bottle, and washed the concoction down in one mouthful.

He opened his holdall and carefully lifted out the folded black uniform with matching black beret and placed them on the bed. He stared at the badge on the beret, gold and red with crossed daggers covered by a bat.

He dressed, put on his black steel toed boots, and carefully placed the beret on his head. He stood and admired his new pristine look in the mirror. The old scruffy traveller now banished to the incinerator along with any traces of Matis and his crew.

He lifted the flap of material on his arm, admired the Russian flag for a few moments, then pressed the flap down securing it with Velcro. He stood and took a final look at himself, proud of the red and gold on the beret badge contrasting with the complete black uniform.

He returned to the lower floor and the electronics room. Two additional male GRU agents had now joined the original team members. They stood to salute him which he ignored, proceeding instead directly to Khristina, "What do you have for me?"

Khristina admired his new look, the uniform compensating for his battered face, "Sir. The last calls made to numbers in Sweden included one to Stockholm and another to an area in the far north, in Lapland. I traced the Stockholm number on our database. It belongs to a petty criminal who deals in stolen goods. I downloaded additional information about him from the Interpol server. The other..."

Petrikov held up his hand to interrupt her then turned to the three men, "Make yourselves busy. I want to know everything about this petty criminal."

The petrified look on the faces of the three agents acknowledged his seniority. In submission they nodded and quickly busied themselves.

He turned to the young woman, "Go on, continue…you said something about the second number."

"Sir. The second number, the one saved under the name Lars, was to a person in Lapland, near the town of Kiruna. I can't give you an exact location, only an approximate point between the nearby mobile network towers. To get an improved understanding of the area I checked our satellite images. It's barren land with a few towns and mining operations. Mostly iron ore mines, a mixture of active and abandoned ones. The phone is currently switched off but if it's reactivated, I'll know immediately."

"Good, ensure that you record any calls and pass them on to me immediately. In the meantime, I need to know more about this Lars person. Can you access the telephone records for his number and trace who he has been talking to?"

"Yes sir, that's possible however it'll take me sometime to create the computer code required to circumvent the telecoms company firewall and get into the records."

"No problem. I need to make some phone calls anyway. We'll talk when I return. And Khristina?"

"Yes Sir?"

"Good work. Come to my room later and we can discuss your computer work in greater detail."

Roslakova raised an eyebrow while Petrikov left the room.

Chapter 18
Början

Activity had increased at the facility. The volunteers who passed the induction process now arriving in groups of eight and taking up their allocated stations within the facility. Along with vans containing volunteers, delivery vans also made regular trips from the processing centre at Umea airport.

Deliveries of equipment, supplies and seeds. The volume of seed parcels was overwhelming. The volunteers began working around the clock to decontaminate, analyse, identify, and classify the seeds before moving them into storage. The result of a Twitter campaign to collect and save the worlds plant species from pollution and overpopulation. Seeds that would restart the vegetation after the biological weapon.

Lars sat at his desk and contemplated the days ahead. The task of setting up the facility and the coordination of transporting the device to India weighed on his mind.

A secretary entered the room and passed him a report with the latest figures. He shook his head when he realised that only thirty eight percent of applicants managed to pass the first phase of tests, a mixture of eco-warriors, climate activists and environmental campaigners. The others, while knowledgeable about the current climate change issues, did not possess the mental health and physical skills required to be suitable.

The successful candidates did not know the real reason they were getting locked inside for two years. Giving out that information before implementation of the weapon would have two detrimental effects. First, the plan would quickly appear on social media and immediately fail. And secondly, to protect the volunteers from the devastating news of the future genocide of all life. To handle that sort of news they would need exceptional mental strength.

He looked at the current stock figures of seeds. They now had over eighty percent of the original plant strains they had sought, plus over one thousand new unclassified seeds.

He threw the reports on his desk and considered the task of formulating a plan to ship the device to the north of India. Shipping by sea in a container from Stockholm to Mumbai then across the country by truck would take up to four weeks, time that increased the chances of the authorities discovering the device. Shipping by air freight would reduce the timescale to three days but it was unlikely to pass airport security in an assembled state. The device would require dismantling into the individual component parts then reassembled on site to avoid discovery. That option required Molantra and he would create problems once he realised the truth. The risks of sending the device to India seemed too high. *Why not select a European city that allowed transport by road? Saint Petersburg, Istanbul, and Naples all have big problems with pollution. Or what about using it in one of the problem cities in Ukraine or Poland? Maybe I can get her to change her mind, get her to consider the alternative options.*

Lars leaned back in his chair. Despite the challenges he still felt happy, soon he would be able to spend all his time with her. She wouldn't have the distractions that she does now. No more worrying about what other people around the world were doing. There would be more time available for her to dedicate to him, especially now that the other two were dead. The longer they spent in seclusion together the more opportunities there would be for him to court her. Overtime, she would learn to love him.

Molantra walked down the corridor from his room and watched as the new recruits began filing into the facility. He arrived at the laboratory and spoke to the chemist, "Who are all these new people?"

She replied in a whisper, "I spoke to some young women at the canteen, new arrivals from Australia. When I asked, they said they've signed up for an experiment on sustainable living. Up to two years isolation with no contact with the outside world. They told me that while helping to keep the facility maintained they would receive training in different fields like Environmental Sciences, Agriculture and Biology. It seems to me that they've been brainwashed into believing it's going to be some fantastic new life."

Molantra declared, "This place is starting to sound more like a cult than an experiment." He pointed at the device he had created and added, "And why do they need that?" He knew the answer already but refused to believe it.

Lars walked into the laboratory and growled, "Tomorrow the biological substance will arrive. You'll have only a day to complete your work. Be ready!"

The two scientists busied themselves doing nothing of any real value while he stood and watched. After several minutes he grew bored and walked away leaving them to their tasks.

His thoughts moved to the young woman computer operator. He walked from the research sector in tunnel seven to the main concourse and proceeded down tunnel five to the IT sector. He walked past the banks of computer servers and other electronic equipment and found her working in a small office by herself.

He sat on the edge of her desk. She looked up at him and he smiled. She blushed and looked at the computer screen. He leaned forward and brushed the hair from her forehead, "You spend too much time sitting at that computer. A beautiful young woman like you should also have some time set aside for fun. Would you like me to show you the rest of the facility?"

She ignored his advances and sharply replied, "I'm happy surrounded by the computers. I don't need to see the facility."

Offended by her rebuke he stood up and hissed, "Very well! Tell me about Sudov. What have you discovered?"

"I've accessed lots of different servers and databases on the internet but unfortunately I can't find any mention of that name. There are no records of a person called Sudov flying into Helsinki or any of the other Finnish airports. The same for the ferry ports. He could have driven across the border or already have been in Finland. I checked all the main hotels and the only booking that exists is the one at the Regent Hotel. He used false papers to check in, I suspect the passport is a fake. I'm sorry but it looks like a dead-end."

Lars considered her response, "What about the police records? They must have found his body and raised a crime report."

"No crime has been reported involving someone with that name."

"What?" Lars was unable to hide the surprise in his voice. He was sure that the Russian was dead. He couldn't have survived, unless someone helped him? He dismissed the concern, "Never mind, I'll contact Matis, I am sure he'll have contacts in the local police."

"Matis?"

"Yes, that's my contact in Helsinki."

"I found this when I was checking on Helsinki news." She brought up the website of an online newspaper. Lars read the headlines, 'Three dead in jewellery store robbery'. He continued to read the article, skimming over most of it, picking out the relevant parts - 'Matis, local crime boss among dead' - 'young woman also missing'.

The individual parts of the information formed in Lars's mind. He stormed out of the small office into the corridor, punching the wall as he spat out the name, "Sudov!"

He rushed to the far end of the IT sector and looked for the maintenance room door attached to the ventilation shaft. After keying in the door lock keycode, he ventured inside and shut the door behind him. He looked up to the top of ventilation shaft five, a circular shaft with a series of tubes, cables and a ladder that led to a hatch at the top. He made quick work of the hundred and twenty feet of ladder, a journey he had made many times before. The sound of air rushing through the ventilation pipes grew louder as he approached the top.

After wrapping one arm around a rung to secure his body he used his free hand to throw open the inspection hatch leading into the machine room. Once inside the small room the noise from the ventilation fan rotating in the large stainless tube became intense.

The construction of seven ventilation shafts with high specification air scrubbers was a major requirement of the mine conversion, essential to provide clean air for the facility during the two-year isolation period. Bergqvist insisted that each of the seven sectors of the new mine layout had independent ventilation to allow for the possibility of sealing off sectors if required. Each of the shafts ran up the inside of the mine exiting on the mountainside to an outlet built of reinforced concrete, camouflaged, and hidden from view. During normal operation large fans at the top of the shaft provided fresh

145

air to the joining sector. If the system detected contaminated outside air a high spec air scrubber system activated to recirculate the internal air instead.

The code panel on the outer hatch flashed a red warning light which he ignored while typing in the override code. The lock beeped and the deadbolts holding the hatch sprung open. He stuck his head out then continued up the ladder until he stood on the ventilation shaft air intake pad, a ten-foot square reinforced concrete block with a five-foot square metal grille in the middle that contained a fan blade. The painted concrete provided maximum camouflage to ensure the intake pad blended in with the surrounding area.

Ventilation shaft five, high on the mountainside, was regularly used by Lars for his private moments. It provided access to a mobile signal and a perfect three-hundred-and-sixty-degree view of the landscape. Below he could see the access road leading to the mine entrance, the town of Kiruna in the distance on his right and the mounds of iron ore mine tailings scattered all around, the waste from years of stripping the mineral from the earth. How fitting that this should be where the revolution would begin.

Chapter 19
Akkajaure Lake

Despite the low light quality, Finn could see the side of the large converted hunting lodge to his left, shaped like a wedge with a sloping, grass covered, roof which merged into the embankment at the rear. At the front, which faced directly onto the lake, there was a ground floor that extended out past the end of the roof. The large veranda on top of the extension contained typical patio furniture, chairs tables and umbrellas.

Built from stacked logs, the lodge looked like most others that he had seen scattered around the lake sides on his hovercraft journey, apart from the size. The proportions of every aspect of the design were bigger, a statement, underlining the fact that the owner was wealthy.

He grabbed the assault rifle from the hovercraft and rushed from the lake shore to a group of trees that provided an advantageous view of the whole house. He took out his powered binoculars and reviewed the full area, scanning from left to right.

He found a separate garage building at the rear of the main house. Positioned at the end of the access road, thirty feet away from, and at ninety degrees to, the main building. He analysed the area, finding no security devices fitted on the rear of the garage. Seeing an opportunity to get closer to the house and remain undetected, he continued through the trees until he was directly behind the garage. Behind a tree trunk he took a final look for danger then ran the thirty yards of open ground to the rear wall. He moved around the perimeter of the building until he was on the side. When he arrived at the front corner he found the garage open and occupied by two vehicles, a red Range Rover Sport, and a four-by-four off road buggy. Using his iBOW, he quickly photographed the vehicle license plates then fitted a magnetic tracker under the rear wheel arch of the Range Rover.

He remained crouched on the inner wall of the garage, looked towards the main house, and considered the open ground between the two. At the rear of the building, he noticed a doorway leading, he assumed, to a basement. He checked the area again for security devices, finding three cameras that would impede his progress. The first camera above him on the front of the garage protected the access road and area between the house and garage. The second was above the basement door covering the access staircase. The third was at the rear of the house covering the main entrance doorway.

He used the stacked log construction of the garage wall to easily climb up onto the grass roof. The grass was damp from the moisture in the evening air. He crawled to the front edge of the garage roof and slowly moved the security camera reducing the field of view.

With the open ground now unprotected he climbed down from the garage roof and ran across to the side of the main building. He edged along the wall until he was near the basement door and directly below the camera. He used the barrel of the assault rifle to slowly push the camera away until it was no longer covering the basement steps.

At the basement door he picked the lock and entered a dark room. Cursing himself for leaving the night vision goggles in the hovercraft, he waited until his eyes adjusted to the poor light conditions. Gradually his vision improved and he spotted a staircase in the corner of the room. Taking slow methodical steps, he moved through the room towards the stairs feeling his way as he went.

*Clang...Bang...*A tin of some kind spun across the floor in front of him and hit something.

He froze and waited for any sounds that would indicate activity above responding to the noise. *Nothing.*

Feeling safe he began moving again.

*Crash...*A set of skis propped against the wall fell in a heap at his feet. He cursed his luck and pushed on until he reached the staircase. Looking up he discovered a door above with light escaping from the gaps around it. He gently climbed the wooden stairs.

*Creak...*He shook his head in disbelief and considered giving up and just announcing his presence. A few more steps and he arrived at the door. Placing his ear to the wooden panel he waited, listened then smiled. *Nothing.*

He picked the lock, slowly opened the door, and entered a large open plan kitchen. An interior designer's dream, like the kitchens he'd seen in magazines. A kitchen for the rich and famous. A wry grin appeared on his face as he imagined himself making beans on toast, the opulence wasted on him.

149

He crept from the kitchen into a large lounge with glass doors all down one side leading out onto the veranda. The décor told him that the place had a woman's touch. Large and contemporary furniture made to the latest designer styles, white and clean. An oversized TV took up most of the space on the far wall in front of a large L-shaped sofa and coffee table. A large reindeer skin took up the space on the wall nearest to him. The room also included a large glass dining table with eight chairs and a telescope near the glass doors.

Below the animal skin a long gloss white wall unit with various cupboard doors and drawers gained his attention. A possible source of information on the person who lived at the house.

He leaned forward and slowly pulled on a door handle. *Smash...*

❖ ❖ ❖ ❖

Finn woke when the cold water hit his face. He moved to wipe the water away, only to realise that gaffer tape held his arms down onto the chair. He tried to move his legs, finding the same. With water running from his head into his eyes he looked around the floor in front of him. On his left he noticed a smashed vase, the reason his head hurt. He continued to scope the area around his feet, unable to lift his head without causing pain in his neck. He stopped when he found a pair of women's legs directly in front of him.

Intrigued, he fought the pain and glanced upwards. His eyes picked out the shape of a young woman with short blonde hair. No doubt the person who had used the broken vase, inducing the pain in his head. He gave his eyes time to focus on the figure.

Her face was a picture, the sort of picture you find in the sort of magazines that advertise perfume. Her natural beauty, pale complexion and bright blue eyes gave her a look sought after by millions of women around the world. Unable to contain himself he moved his head lower finding her slim body covered by a skin tight, black Lycra bodysuit, on her feet black trainers.

Her dress style left nothing to the imagination but that did not stop Finn's mind trying. The contours of her body told him that she was not wearing any underwear, top or bottom. She may as well have been standing in front of him naked, at least that's what Finn wanted.

As his eyes returned to her face, he recognised her as the woman in the YouTube videos, Agneta Bergqvist.

She leaned forward, slapped him hard across the face, "Your eyes give away your thoughts. Who are you?"

Finn grinned and quipped, "I'm the man you've always dreamt of meeting."

She hit him again, harder, "Very funny but we'll see how quickly your humour changes. I won't ask you again, who are you?"

"It's hard to get in touch with you. I was hoping to arrange a date, are you available tonight? We can maybe get a table at a local restaurant, have a meal and a chat, share a bottle of wine, then return here for a nightcap. What do you think?"

Creak. Finn turned to his left and discovered a man holding an assault rifle standing immediately behind him. His senses began to return, he looked towards the other end of the room and found another armed man. Continuing with his performance he joked, "What's all this? Just so you know I'm not into anything kinky. I'm sure we'll be able to make enough sweet music on our own."

She stepped back and gestured to the man standing behind him. The guard placed his assault rifle against the wall and walked around to face Finn. A grin appeared on the guard's face, Finn raised his eyebrows and the guard punched him on the left side of his face. The guard followed up with a blow to the right and another to the left. Finn's head rocked form side to side with the blows causing more pain in his neck.

A cut appeared on Finn's left eyebrow, through gritted teeth he said, "Look shithead if you want to get rough, I'm all for it. Just untie my hands and we'll see how brave you really are."

Bergqvist laughed and the guard followed up with another left and right combination to the face and then a final blow to the stomach.

Finn gasped. The breath forced from his lungs with the force of the final blow. Through gritted teeth he spluttered, "Do that again and you'll regret it."

The man followed up with two more blows to the head. Blood began to run from Finn's nose and a cut on his lip.

He began feeling light headed and shook his head to stop himself passing out.

Bergquist shouted, "You're dressed like a soldier and have a British accent. Why are you following me? Why involve yourself in my business?"

"If I tell you then I'll have to kill you and you're too pretty for that to happen. Unlike your meatball friend here."

"Why were you at Yacheyka?"

"By the way I forgot to ask, how's the shoulder healing?"

Bergqvist moved her hand to the wound, "A lucky shot from an opportunistic thief."

"Thief?"

"That's why you and your friend were there, isn't it? To steal things from the bank. Picking over the corpses of those unfortunate humans."

"You know why I'm here. Why don't you just hand it over."

Bergqvist realised that he was talking about the bio-weapon and glanced towards a picture on the wall.

Finn noted the look, "Is that where the safe is? Why don't you just give me the stuff and get out of here while you can. I promise to count to fifty and give you a head start."

Bergqvist ignored the request while Finn turned to the guard, "You can stay shithead! We've got business to settle."

After a few moments silence Bergqvist walked over to the picture, opened it like a door, revealing a safe with a digital screen and retinal scanner. She typed in an eight-digit code and placed her head in the scanner. With a loud clunk the safe unlocked. She snapped the lock handle down and opened the heavy metal door. Inside Finn could see various documents, a jewellery case, bundles of money and a small silver case. She reached in and carefully removed the case, placing it on the coffee table. After snapping the latches, she opened the small case and showed Finn the contents, a row of seven test tubes containing blue liquid, "You want me to give you this?"

"I'd be happier if you just locked it away again."

She put the case on the coffee table and removed one test tube. She shook it and said, "Only humanity could have the desire to create something that can kill everything, even themselves. If the Russians had managed to mass produce this, they could have wiped out all life on the planet in an instance. Over the last seventy years humans have been doing that gradually anyway with global warming and environmental damage. I will speed up the process, my scientists are already working on translating the documents. With these samples I will make enough to wipe humans from the Earth."

"You mean apart from you and your merry band of eco-terrorists?"

She shook her head in disbelief at Finn's analysis of her dream. In disgust she replaced the test tube in the case and locked the latches and said, "The earth will recover, our ancestors will reseed it in future years and live a simple life as it was in the beginning."

"The climate activist turned into humankind's judge and jury? The eco-terrorist in sexy Lycra. The elfin faced harbinger of doom. What happened to turn such a beautiful and privileged young woman into a total life hating bitch? Did you get dropped on your head as a baby?"

She reacted angrily, "Shut up! You know nothing about me."

"That's why I'm here, I'd like to get to know you in greater detail. Why don't you put that nasty stuff away, take off these straps, pour me a glass of wine and you can tell me all about yourself."

While talking Finn continued to exert pressure on the gaffer tape by moving his arms backwards, forwards and side to side. Each motion stretching the tape and loosening the adhesive grip.

Bergqvist ignored his comments and began picking up the pieces of broken vase. Seeing her bending over in front of him, he quickly forgot about the tape, "Was it valuable?"

"A relic of ancient times when people lived in harmony with the environment. Only cutting down trees or killing animals to supplement their lives, not for sport or profit."

She straightened and threw the pottery pieces into a small wicker basket, "You still haven't answered my questions. I'm losing my patience with you. It appears that this is just a joke to you. I think it's time we focus your mind." She gestured to the guard.

He picked up a lamp, tore the electrical cable from the base then took a knife and stripped away the insulation exposing the bare copper wires inside. He twisted one wire around Finn's left wrist, the other around his right. The guard plugged the lead into an extension cable and looked at Bergqvist.

She looked at Finn, "For the last time, who are you?"

Finn growled, "Do your worst sicko."

She nodded, signalling to the guard to switch on the power. Electrical current began to flow through the cable, the electrons seeking a route to ground. Entering at one wrist they rushed up Finn's arm, through his chest cavity and down the other arm. His body became instantly paralysed, every sinew contracted as the electrical current activated the muscles. He gritted his teeth, unable to open his mouth, jerking his head backwards and forwards in agony. She nodded and the guard turned off the power.

Finn's body began to relax but the muscle pain remained. Realising the time for joking was over he began working on the tape again.

She leaned forward and shouted in his face, "Talk before I tell him to leave it switched on long enough to kill you. What's your name? Who do you work for?"

Finn quipped, "They say that electricity is more environmentally friendly, so you should at least be happy with your torture methods."

She sighed in frustration, straightened then nodded to the guard. The electrical current racked his body, the force giving him the extra strength to break the gaffer tape on his right arm. He pulled his hand upwards, ripping the cable from his wrist and disconnecting the flow of current. With his free hand he tore the cable from his left wrist. The guard approached, Finn held the live cable up and stuck it into the man's neck. The electrical shock blew the guard backwards onto the floor away from the assault rifle. Finn instinctively knew he had moments to live and desperately pulled at the tape holding his left arm.

Bergqvist screamed and dived over the back of the sofa, reaching for a pistol on the coffee table. Now with her out of the way the second guard, further away, had a clear view of Finn. He grinned and lifted his assault rifle up.

Finn looked into the man's eyes knowing in a second he would be dead. Suddenly the glass doors leading to the veranda shattered as bullets ripped into the guard, throwing his body to the bedroom doorway. Finn looked to his right and observed a figure moving across the veranda towards the living room. The first guard pulled out a pistol and returned fire towards the shooter. The figure dived for cover behind some patio furniture.

The shooting allowed Finn the extra time to free his arm and he rolled the chair sideways onto the floor, the force breaking the tape on his legs. He crawled along the floor towards the electrocuted guard's assault rifle. Bergqvist picked up the pistol and began shooting at him while the guard pinned down the shooter outside. Finn left the rifle and dived behind the sofa for cover.

Click. The sound told him the guard's magazine was empty. The break in shooting allowed the shooter outside to get up from the floor. Bergqvist shouted something in Swedish and the guard moved towards her, reloading as he moved. From the other side of the sofa the two disappeared into the entrance hall as the person on the veranda began shooting again.

Finn moved for the assault rifle as a figure ran in from outside through the room and into the hallway, following the others. He grabbed the rifle and followed, only for the unknown person to push him back into the room as a grenade went off. The explosion blew the door off its hinges and tore the reindeer skin from the wall, causing it to land on top of Finn. The noise of a car starting outside then driving away at high speed reverberated around the room. The smoke from the grenade began to clear as Finn struggled on the floor with the large animal skin. He heard a loud laugh as someone pulled the heavy skin away from him. He immediately recognised the comedian. *Petrikov.*

He accepted the hand that Petrikov held out to him and the Russian pulled him up from the floor, "You seem to be having trouble with the local wildlife my good friend."

Finn smiled, "Thanks."

His thoughts turned to the biological weapon, he looked to the coffee table. *Shit! She took it!*

In the hallway a small fire broke out which Petrikov quickly stamped on, putting out the flames. He then moved to the kitchen while Finn collected his assault rifle and pistol. Petrikov returned holding a bottle and two small glasses, "Vodka?"

"Too right!" Finn added.

❖ ❖ ❖ ❖

After searching the property and finding nothing of interest the two men moved to the veranda. They slumped down in two sun loungers like tourists on the Costa Blanca. Finn rubbed his face and vowed to get revenge on the guard who beat him.

Petrikov poured two glasses of vodka, handed one to Finn then drank his glass in one go. He looked and waited until Finn had done the same. They sat in silence for several moments both processing what had happened.

While pouring another two glasses Petrikov asked, "So what brings you all the way out here my friend? The last time we met you were on the trail of the people who had taken stuff from Yacheyka."

"I was just about to ask the same. I thought you were off to the Caribbean. What happened?"

"I'm on the trail of a Swede. And you?"

"The same!"

"Judging by your uniform you are not just the relative of a fisherman."

Petrikov laughed, "True."

"Which are you? Special forces?"

"Military intelligence, GRU," Petrikov confirmed.

"I'm starting to get the feeling that there's a lot more to your story than I've been told. It's no coincidence that you travelled with me is it? I'm not sure of the connection between you and Mac either. MI6 and the GRU don't generally work together on things. In fact, from what I've seen the two organisations hate each other."

"Hate is a strong word. Consider it more like an old married couple. They get on with each other, help each other when they can but also have their own little secrets and endeavours. I've known Mac for many years. With the full support of our superiors, we help each other on mutual objectives. Take space exploration as an example. Together we share a space station. We also let you use our rockets to get your satellites into space knowing that you'll use them to spy on us."

"It gives me the shivers all that spy craft stuff. What I'm more surprised about is how you managed to turn up here. Don't get me wrong I'm glad that you did."

They finished another glass of vodka before Petrikov replied, "I've been working on bringing down a smuggling ring that has been taking antiques from Russia. They ship the goods into Finland or Estonia using car ferries, then either break them up or sell them on to dealers within Europe or America. A corrupt member of the party set up and ran the organisation after he avoided prosecution. Connections in high places decided to let him leave the country on the warning that he was never to return. The salt mines would have been my choice. While running my investigation, I met up with a Swede who decided to beat me to within an inch of my life."

"You came here to find him?"

"Not quite. We traced his mobile to the Kiruna area but couldn't get an exact fix. To try and find out his identity I asked my staff to start tracing the people he'd been talking to. They managed to trace a number that he regularly calls to this place. I came here to find out who my mystery man was."

Petrikov poured two more glasses of vodka, sat silently for a few moments then asked, "And why are you here?"

"I'm not sure how much I can tell you. I need to speak to Mac to get clearance but it could be to both of our advantages to work together. You're right I'm still on the trail of the people who were at Yacheyka. The woman who lives here took something from the laboratory. We suspect she has the biological weapon, I'm here to recover it. When I last spoke to Mac he said that he was trying to trace one of her accomplices in the Kiruna area. It sounds to me that we're both looking for the same people."

"And you didn't think to tell me about these people stealing Russian property on our trip back to Finland? You said that you didn't find any evidence of them taking anything, we disturbed them before they could do anything, you said that you killed them."

"Look I'm sorry but I didn't have the clearance. You know how MI6 works. There was a third person who got away, they took the biological samples."

"Where's Mac now? Back in England?"

"No, he's here in Finland."

"Good let's go and talk to him. How did you get here? Helicopter? Car?"

"I've got a hovercraft tied up over there on the lake shore."

Petrikov laughed, "A hovercraft? Who do you think you are my friend? James Bond?"

Finn shrugged his shoulders, "James Bond always gets the beautiful women, I'm never that lucky. I'm usually too busy getting shot at or shit on by my superiors."

"It's the business we're in, my English friend."

"Very true."

"Let's get going. Take me to Mac."

Finn grabbed his assault rifle from the table, Petrikov grabbed the bottle of vodka. Together they walked to the hovercraft and Finn repeated the journey back to where he parked the Landcruiser. The morning sun was climbing off the horizon as the two men secured the hovercraft to the trailer and began the drive to Gällivare. Near the safehouse Finn stopped the Toyota on a grass verge, "Wait here, I need to make a call."

Petrikov smiled, "Don't worry my friend I know all about the safehouse. Is Strom still getting bigger?"

Finn looked at the Russian, shrugged his shoulders and restarted the Toyota. He began to wonder if there were other things that the MI6 man and the Russian had decided to keep from him.

Chapter 20
Början

The guard jumped into the driver's seat of the Range Rover Sport, started the engine, and began moving before Bergqvist was fully inside. The vehicle left the garage at high-speed out onto the dirt access road. The force slammed Bergqvist back against the passenger seat causing her to drop the silver case into the footwell. The pair momentarily looked at each other, expecting the worst, but nothing happened. The protection inside the case had served its purpose.

The Rover made easy work of the dirt track, gaining speed quickly. Bergqvist looked behind to make sure no one was following, then cursed, "Shit! Shit! Shit! Who the fuck are those guys? The British man knew about the biological samples. He was trying to steal them from me."

"I don't know boss! But they don't appear to be just a couple of thieves, they're highly trained. My guess is they're special forces or mercenaries working for another organisation who wants the biological material."

"Special forces? Mercenaries? For which organisation? If it's a criminal gang we can only guess why they want the biological material. It is not for the same reasons as us that's for sure. Whoever holds it can blackmail all the world powers? The guy had a British accent. What do the British want with me? And the other one, was that the guy from Helsinki? Lars said that he was a Russian. Britain and

Russian working together? As far as I'm aware they don't have any mutual agreements on a national level. It must be a criminal gang, don't you think?"

The driver did not know the answer. Instead of replying he just shrugged his shoulders and returned his attention to the road.

Bergqvist stared out of the window and calmly said, "We need to move the schedule forward."

∴ ∴ ∴ ∴

The intelligence officer shouted excitedly, "Got it!"

Mac responded, "Where?"

"It's on the road from the lakeside house heading towards Kiruna."

"Kiruna?" Mac walked over to the notice board and looked at the map of the area, "The iron ore mines?"

"It looks like that's where the vehicle is heading. It's traveling towards the other contact that we're tracking up there. They must be planning to meet up."

"What about Finn? Any news?"

"His iBOW indicates that he's still at the lakeside house at Akkajaure."

Mac became concerned, "So we've got no way of knowing if he's in danger? He could have been captured and taken in that vehicle, or worse…dead."

"Do you want me to call his iBOW?"

"No that could blow his cover, we'll just have to wait and see what develops."

⁘ ⁘ ⁘ ⁘

The Range Rover pulled off the single-track paved road onto the dirt track. A fine dust surrounded the vehicle, swirling around the wheels and coating the windows. The morning sun, newly risen began to change the sky from a threatening red to a pale blue. The driver slowed and pulled to the side to allow a delivery van to pass. Bergqvist picked up the silver case and held it on her lap.

At the outer gate the security guard recognised the vehicle and quickly opened it. As the driver pulled up in front of the large steel doors, a guard inside watching on a security camera, pressed a green button. The two large doors slowly opened, driven by hydraulic rams installed in the tunnel roof. Once inside the driver parked the Range Rover and the outer doors closed behind. Bergqvist climbed out, clinging onto the silver case and jumped into the electric buggy. The driver drove to the end of the tunnel.

Bergqvist climbed out and said to the driver, "Use another vehicle and return to my house, there's a body that needs disposing of. While you're there look for evidence those men may have left behind that we can use to trace them."

She completed the decontamination process and walked into the main facility. She was surprised by the number of people occupying the spaces, moving between tunnels, and getting ready for the experiment to start. The occupants all wore the same uniform of white trousers and shirt with green stripes.

Her current appearance all in black Lycra made her stand out and she noticed some staring. Ignoring the attention, she walked across the main concourse towards the accommodation tunnel. Near the entrance a group of young men stopped and began to stare at her. She continued to walk, noticing their eyes following her movement. One made a comment to the others. She placed the small silver case on a table and said to two young women, "Can you please look after this for me." The women nodded to confirm the request.

She then approached the young men, "What are you looking at?"

One of the men eyed her up and down then replied, "Wow you're hot."

She slapped the young man across the face then grabbed his throat and forced him against the wall. With her free hand she grabbed his balls and began squeezing them, "Women here are not sexual objects to be leered at."

As she tightened her grip on his neck and balls, tears appeared in the young man's eyes and he mumbled, "Sorry, I…"

As he began to speak, she released her grip on his neck and punched him hard in the face. He fell unconscious on the floor as the other young men began moving away, blending into the growing crowd.

Two security guards appeared and she ordered, "Get rid of him, his contract is terminated, he's not suitable to be part of our revolution."

As the guards dragged the young man away, she addressed the crowd, "Let that be a lesson to everyone. Now return to your allocated duties."

The crowd parted and Bergqvist walked on, still angry at the way the British man had both spoken and looked at her, like an object, just like those young men.

She eventually arrived at her living quarters and she used the comms system to contact Lars.

"You're here now? You said you'd be coming in the evening."

"There was an incident at my house."

"What happened?

"Come here and I'll tell you about it."

❖ ❖ ❖ ❖

The security guards dragged the young man through the exit tunnel to the outside parking area. As he regained consciousness one of the guards punched him in the back and he fell on his face. The man turned over and began to sit up.

The guard pulled a pistol and aimed it at the young man's head, as he slowly squeezed the trigger a van approached and he quickly stuffed it back into the holster.

The van stopped at the parking area and the latest volunteers began disembarking. As they walked towards the entrance door the security guards acted cool, as if helping the young man to his feet. Seeing an opportunity to escape, the young man pushed the guards away and began running, first heading down the road, then off the side into the wasteland. He began weaving through the mounds of mine tailings until he reached a patch of trees. Diving inside he rolled over onto his front and viewed the area he had run from. In the distance he noticed the two security guards searching, with guns drawn.

The young man pulled himself up and continued to run between the trees, changing direction periodically while maintaining a downward track.

At the tree line the guards gave up looking, ran to the parking area and climbed into a security van. The driver followed the road down the mountainside while the passenger scanned the area for signs of the young man.

The driver spoke, "If he gets away, you do realise that we'll be in deep shit."

The young man continued his journey down the mountainside until he discovered in the distance the junction where the mine access road met the main road into Kiruna. A large service area, beyond the junction, offered the possibility of sanctuary with a petrol station, motel, and restaurant area.

He pushed on through the undergrowth until he reached the edge of the main road. Seeing a Början delivery van approaching he hid in a ditch until it passed. After running over the road, he walked between the rows of parked trucks until he found an empty one. Climbing inside, he quickly searched the cab and found a lunchbox with some food. He then reached behind the seat and found a coat.

Through the windscreen he watched the security van pull into the car park. The van parked near the restaurant then the two guards climbed out and began searching between the parked trucks.

He took the coat and food and climbed down from the truck and moved to the truck stop toilet block, avoiding the guards as he went. Pushing past the current occupants, a mixture of truckers and mine workers, he found an empty cubicle. He sat on the toilet and searched the coat for valuables, finding a wallet with ID, cash, and bank cards. He removed the bank notes and stuffed them into his trouser pocket. He quickly ate the food then discarded the coat, wallet, and lunchbox onto the floor.

He listened as the guards entered the toilet block and another voice growled at them, "You're with those freaks up the mountain who want to close all the mines down."

One of the guards responded, "Look, we don't want any trouble, we're looking for a young man. Did he come in here?"

Another voice grunted, "Looking for a young man? Your type's not welcome here. Get out!"

He listened as the truckers pushed the security guards towards the doorway and out into the car park. Hearing a scuffle taking place outside, the young man left the cubicle and made his way outside. Seeing the guards preoccupied by a group of truckers pushing them around, he proceeded undetected to a new hiding place behind a truck. In the distance he noticed the entrance to the motel. After deciding that it was best to lay low, he ran over and purchased a room with the stolen money. In the room he watched from the window as the truckers gave the security guards a beating outside.

The two guards put up a fight, trading blows, but soon realised they were fighting a losing battle. In desperation the driver shouted, "Come on let's get out of here."

They ran to the security van while the jubilant truckers shouted insults and threw beer cans and bottles. Once secure inside the van the driver started the engine and drove out of the carpark at speed. He turned to the passenger who was nursing a broken nose, "Get your story straight, after a chase we killed and buried the guy in the woods."

"And how do you explain what's happened to us?"

"We've had trouble with the locals before, we'll just tell it like it is."

❖ ❖ ❖ ❖

The intelligence officer looked at Mac, "Sir."

"Yes?"

"Finn is on the move. He's currently moving on the lake about half way back to where he parked the vehicle."

Mac looked at his watch, "Zero six hundred. He should be here within the next couple of hours. We need to debrief him and find out what he's discovered."

❖ ❖ ❖ ❖

Bergqvist sat up on the bed when she heard the room bell ring. Walking over to the door she looked at the small TV screen showing the tall blonde-haired man standing outside. She opened the door, "Lars, come in, we've got much to talk about."

Lars entered the room and held up a bottle of Pinot Noir, "Fancy a drink?"

Bergqvist looked at the digital clock next to the bed, "It's barely one in the afternoon and your mind is on drinking?"

"I thought it would give us an opportunity to relax and consider our next move, together. I've got some concerns about the location that's been chosen." Lars pulled a corkscrew from his back pocket and uncorked the bottle. He walked over to a small table and poured two fingers of wine into a couple of beaker style glasses, handing one to Bergqvist. She took the glass, swilled the contents around then smelt the contents.

Lars prompted her, "Do you remember it?"

She shook her head, showing no real interest in where the question was leading, then drank the glass in one, "Tell me about your concerns."

"I've checked all of the options and India is just too far to guarantee a successful outcome. It offers too many opportunities to fail. The journey alone could expose our plan long before we get a chance to it off the ground."

"Okay, so what's your suggestion?"

171

He refilled her glass while continuing to talk, "I think we should consider a large European city? There are many that generate high levels of pollution. For instance, I was hoping you'd consider Naples, Istanbul, or personal choice Saint Petersburg. There are so many positives that make it suitable. We can travel by car ferry out of the port at Stockholm. With the device in the vehicle and under our control there's much less chance of detection. The customs and border guards will be easy to bribe. Plus, it means we send the first message to the country that produced the biological weapon in the first place. Quite ironic don't you think?".

"Okay, I agree. We'll change the location to Saint Petersburg."

Lars put his glass down and said coyly, "You look stressed my darling."

The comment infuriated Bergqvist. She banged the glass down on the table and some of the wine splashed down the front of her white towelling dressing gown, "Don't darling me! Am I the only person who's concerned about the two men that are following me?"

Lars moved forward and placed his hands on the lapels of the dressing gown and began opening them, revealing her breasts. Bergqvist raised a knee into his groin and he fell at her feet. She pulled the dressing gown closed and walked away.

Lars struggled to his feet, grasping at his injured groin and mumbled, "Tell me exactly what happened at your house then."

"The Englishman who killed Nils and Patrik broke in but we managed to capture him. He activated the infra-red perimeter sensors outside, triggering the silent alarm in the house. I told the guards to allow him to enter so we could capture and interrogate him. After some persuasion he revealed his interest in the biological weapon. He's followed us from Yacheyka to our offices in Stockholm and now to my home. I can only assume that we've got competition that sees the monetary value in owning the weapon."

With the pain easing he asked, "Where's this Englishman now?"

"He escaped with help from his Russian friend. I thought you said that he was dead."

"I was sure that he was, but it appears that someone must have helped him. I've just discovered myself that he's responsible for the deaths of the petty criminals in Helsinki who helped find him. I'm unsure of the connection between these two men but they seem to have the resources to cause us problems. You're right to consider moving the scheduled date forward."

Bergqvist calmed down and approached him, "I'm sorry for my little outburst, will it still function?"

A grin appeared on his face, "Maybe with some tenderness?"

She turned away and ignored his response, "Your suggestion of a location which is closer seems to fit in with our need to activate our plan early. We'll be able to deploy the device within a matter of the days. How are the engineers progressing with the device development?"

Lars nodded, "It's ready. They just need the biological sample."

"Good!" She said excitedly. "I want it ready by tomorrow morning."

Bergqvist opened a safe on the wall and took out the small silver case. She removed one test tube and held it up in front of him, "Here it is. The answer to all of our dreams." She replaced the test tube, locked up the case and passed it to him, "Take this to the chemist, make sure she removes one test tube only then lock the case in the laboratory safe."

"Where's the key for the safe?"

"It's a digital key. I'll open the safe from here using my computer once you are ready, call me. And make sure that the you don't allow them to handle the substance until the laboratory door is properly sealed, we can't afford any accidents."

She picked up the wine bottle, topped up her glass then removed her dressing gown. Lars watched as it fell to the floor. He looked at her naked body with a mixture of lust and love in his eyes.

She drank some of the wine and calmly said, "When you return from the laboratory you can make love to me, it'll be your last opportunity. The issue of these men is troubling me. To ensure our plan does not fail I've decided that you must go with the device to ensure its deployment."

"I thought you wanted me to stay here with you? I thought that we were starting a new life together. If I'm with the device how do I get back inside here once it is activated?"

"We'll worry about that later. I need you to do this for me, I can't trust anyone else to do it...my love." She moved towards the bed, "Now hurry before I change my mind."

Lars clutched the silver case and hurried to the laboratory. Molantra and the chemist heard the door opening, turning from their workstation to see him pass through the airlock. They hid their disappointment when he held up the silver case and announced, "It's here. You can finish the project."

Lars placed the silver case on the workstation counter top and opened the latches revealing the seven test tubes. He advised caution, "Remove one tube only and make sure you handle it with extreme care. If you drop or spill any of the liquid, we'll all die, instantly."

The chemist and Molantra exchanged a look of horror at hearing the comment. Reluctantly the chemist took one test tube from the case and carefully transferred it to a draw on a sealed biohazard cabinet. She pressed a button transferring the test tube to the inside of the unit. She placed her hands into the flexible rubber arms on the front of the unit. With her left hand she moved the test tube to a stand in the middle of the unit. With her right she picked up a beaker of liquid.

"What are you doing?" Lars enquired.

"In order for the biological agent to be dispersed as a mist we must first reduce the viscosity by diluting it. To do that we use a chemically inert solution that will preserve the original biological agent and not harm it."

"Fine, continue with your work. How long will it take until the dispersion device is ready?"

Molantra interrupted, "We can't rush these things. You want the device to function reliably, don't you? We'll need at least another twenty-four hours to create the solution and to transfer it to the gas bottles."

Lars looked at his watch, "I get the impression that you're stalling. Do I need to remind you of the consequences of failure? Make sure it is ready by one o'clock tomorrow afternoon. Any later and both of you suffer the consequences."

Lars left the room, he had other more exciting things on his mind. Hurrying along the corridor he decided it was best to give Bergqvist the news of the delay afterwards.

Chapter 21
Gällivare

Finn pulled the Toyota Landcruiser into the safehouse garage. Petrikov helped him to disconnect and store the Hovercraft trailer back to its original position. The pair descended the stairs and walked along the corridor to the comms room, finding Mac and the team still working.

"You made it then!" Mac announced. "And I see that you've brought a companion with you."

Finn patted Petrikov on the back and declared, "If it hadn't been for this guy, I'd probably be lying in a shallow grave now."

"You look like you've also had a bit of a beating, trouble with the woman?" Mac quipped.

"She's certainly feisty," Finn said.

Mac pointed to the empty chairs on the other side of the table, "Take a seat guys we need to go over what you've found and where we go from here."

The two men sat down and Finn described in detail what had taken place at Bergqvist's house.

"You actually saw the biological samples?" Mac asked.

"How would I know? I'm not a chemist. What I saw was a small case, like the one at Yacheyka, with seven test tubes containing a blue liquid. The case had space for eight tubes. We can assume that the missing one is smashed on the lab floor in Russia."

"Well at least it looks like she still has all of the remaining samples. The other problem we must consider is the data on the formulation of the germ. If she hands that on to someone else, they could start replicating it and we will lose control of the situation. It's imperative that we urgently get the samples and the formula."

Finn nodded in agreement, "We know she has the samples and she said that her scientists were decoding the documents. I need to capture Bergqvist and I'm not doing that sitting around here talking to you. Did you pick up the signal from the tracking device I activated?"

One of the intelligence officers spoke up, "We followed the signal to a mine on the outskirts of the town of Kiruna, about seventy-five miles from here. Then it disappeared off the map, we think the vehicle has driven into the mine, blocking the signal."

Finn continued, "That could be our opportunity to resolve this. If she's gone into hiding in the mine, we can capture her, secure the biological material, and get all the data in one swoop. What do we know about this mine?"

"It used to belong to Urmina, her father's company. When the iron ore ran out Urmina sold it to Existence on the cheap. The sale agreement stipulated that Existence would clean up the surrounding area by landscaping the mine tailings and replanting trees. Despite making that agreement a few years ago there's not been much evidence of any clean-up work taking place. Official statements and PR responses from Existence have all responded to that question with the fact that they're first making the interior of the mine safe."

"Is that true?" Petrikov asked.

"It's true that they've been doing lots of work inside but getting any solid information on what's actually happening in there is impossible. It seems they only work within their own circle of contacts, shippers, contractors etc. Businesses that are sympathetic to the cause…protecting the environment. I searched a few of the shipping databases and found lots of shipments for Existence going into the seaport at Luleå." The blank faces of the men sitting around the table told him they did not have a clue so he added, "It's the nearest port, two hundred miles from the mine."

"What sort of goods are they shipping into the place?" Finn asked.

The intelligence officer picked up some papers on the desk and read aloud, "The customs documents cover all manner of things. Generators, steel beams, air ducts, computers, lab equipment, beds, chairs, tables, plates, cups, lighting, electronics, hydroponics equipment, sun lamps. Like I said all sorts. If you're asking me, they're fitting the place out ready to move in.

"Any evidence of the buying and shipping of weapons?" Mac asked."

"I've not seen anything. I don't have a lot of confidence in what's written on the customs documents. I've found the names of a couple of port officials in among the accounts records we took from the Existence computer server."

"They could be building a bloody fortress in there for all we know," Mac remarked.

Finn interrupted, "Hang on you've lost me! I thought you said that the father was mining uranium? Surely it's not that easy to convert the place?"

The officer continued, "This area of Sweden has many different minerals. When prospecting for uranium it's normal to find seams of other valuable ores. They discovered that the area around Kiruna holds large reserves of iron ore. Uranium mining takes place further north and south of here."

"Well at least that's comforting," Petrikov joked.

"How do we get in there then? What have you found out on access points and vulnerabilities?" Finn urged.

"We know next to nothing. We can't use a drone as technically we're not supposed to be here. The area is very remote and we don't have any local resources that we can call on for intel. What we really need is someone on the ground gathering intel on what's really happening there."

Finn looked at Mac, "So when do I go?"

Petrikov replied, "We'll go together my friend, after we've eaten some food."

"Why are you so interested in this place? You need to get back to your side of the fence," Mac retorted.

"Don't worry Mac, I'm not here to get involved in your caper. You seem to have all our interests at heart. I don't want that biological weapon falling into the wrong hands either and that includes Russian ones." Petrikov moved uneasily in his chair as he remembered his damaged groin, the heavy material of his black GRU uniform causing unwelcome pressure. Through gritted teeth he added, "I've got a score to settle with a Swedish man. I was closing in on him when I encountered the woman torturing our friend here. We appear to be after the same people. I'll go along with your plan and support where I can but let me warn you both. If my Swedish friend is there, he's mine, no one else touches him."

Finn noted the look of pain on the Russian's face and the determination in his voice then looked at Mac, "I'm happy with that. If we're to blend in up there I'll need someone with me who knows the area and culture."

"You can take Strom for that, he's Swedish." Mac climbed from his chair and began pacing the room, "I must admit I'm a little uneasy about your involvement Petrikov. We go back a long time together and you've always been straight with me. I cannot thank you enough for helping me in the past including what you did to get Finn inside Russia but, at the end of the day, you're still Russian."

Petrikov shrugged his shoulders, "Fine! If I'm not wanted, I'll still be going there by myself and it appears that you need me more than I need you."

The Russian motioned to get up and Finn grabbed his arm, "You guys can sort this crap out later. Our priority now is finding that biological weapon before they start sharing it out to different people, or worse, use it. I need Petrikov with me, end of discussion."

Mac held his hands up in submission, "Okay, fine go together but I'm still in charge of this mission and you report to me before you do anything." He looked at Petrikov and added, "And that includes you too Vanya!"

Finn blurted out, "Vanya?"

"And what sort of name is Kirkland?" Petrikov asked.

Mac groaned, "Come on guys this is serious."

Petrikov held up his hands, "Fine, you're the boss Mac but the Swede is still mine."

Chapter 22
Kiruna Truck Stop

Finn and Petrikov changed into civilian clothes, allowing them to blend in with the locals. Strom made a couple of false ID cards. Not perfect copies but good enough to fool a local police officer. They agreed on taking hand weapons, hiding pistols in their inside jacket pockets.

Finn programmed the coordinates of the mine into the GPS application and looked at his watch. *12.56.* The planned route showed seventy-two miles and a journey time of just over one and half hours.

As the two men climbed into the Landcruiser Finn declared, "We don't want any shooting remember. This is a fact-finding mission."

Petrikov nodded in agreement.

Finn noticed that the Russian sitting uncomfortably in the passenger seat, "Are you okay? You look like you're in pain. Were you injured back there at the house?"

Petrikov took out his next ration of tablets and a vodka bottle from his rucksack. Washing them down with a big gulp of liquid he said, "It's nothing that a few tablets and beating the hell out a Swede won't rectify."

Finn smirked, taking some twisted pleasure in the Russian's pain, "I thought you had a touch of the blue balls mate. I was going to suggest we stop off at a brothel on the way to get you fixed up."

"It'll be a long time before I can think of such pleasures my friend."

Finn started the diesel engine and followed the dirt track from the safehouse onto the tarmac road. He drove on the road towards the airport and joined the E10, the only road with a decent road surface. The road swept north through a landscape of scrubland, forest, and large areas of water, deeper into Lapland.

As the road neared the town of Kiruna Finn noticed an increase in traffic, mostly mining trucks hauling iron ore from the mines in the area. The GPS indicated a turn approaching on the left. Instead of taking the road Finn slowed down and pulled into the truck stop on the right.

"Why have you stopped?" Petrikov asked.

"The GPS says we need to head up the dirt track over there to the mine. If we drive to the entrance and there's security in place we'll just give ourselves away. Let's wait down here for a while and watch who's using the road. Once it starts to get dark then we'll make our way to the mine on foot...via the woods."

"Seems like a sensible plan, we can also get something to eat and drink."

"Of course," Finn declared.

Finn moved the Landcruiser to the front of the truck stop diner and parked. He grinned when he noticed that the 'S' on the blue neon sign was faulty leaving just "unset Bar" on the window. He looked at Petrikov and the two men laughed.

On the dashboard Finn noticed the outside temperature had dropped around five degrees from the maximum of ten earlier in the day. They climbed out of the vehicle and put on their coats and hats.

Petrikov headed inside to secure a table next to the window while Finn walked around outside. Regular large trucks pulled in with truckers requiring fuel, to rest, use the toilet or restaurant facilities. Other vehicles, mostly four by fours and SUVs also came and went with workers from the mines.

Standing near a truck he watched as a van pulled into the dirt road opposite and began heading up towards the mine. He waited and another appeared, coming down. The van stopped at the junction waiting for the main road to clear then drove directly across and into the truck stop car park. The driver jumped out and went to the toilet. Finn moved alongside the van then crouched down and fitted a tracker device under the rear bumper.

As he straightened up a trucker appeared alongside the van and said something in Swedish. Finn turned to walk away and the trucker grabbed him by the shoulder. In an instance Finn grabbed the hand, twisted it violently, and pulled the man's arm behind his back. The man shouted out in pain. Another trucker appeared along with the van driver. Finn held the man for a few moments then pushed him away in the direction of the others. The trucker barged into the two men, who, wanting the fight to continue, pushed him towards Finn. The trucker clenched his fist, spun around, and threw a punch into fresh air. As he lost his balance, he noticed Petrikov pulling Finn away towards the diner.

"What happened to blending in?" the Russian quipped.

In the background Finn heard the men shouting, then losing interest and moving away.

In the diner the two men sat together at a booth. Finn sent a message on his iBOW to the intelligence guy to activate the tracker. Petrikov ordered coffees and two plates of reindeer stew. While eating they watched the regular delivery vans taking goods and people up the dirt road towards the Existence mine.

The server, a young man, came over to refill the coffee cups. Petrikov asked the server in broken Swedish if he spoke English. The server shook his head, spoke in Swedish and pointed to a young man sitting at the end of the bar, his head resting on the counter top with a half empty beer glass in his hand. Petrikov handed the server a couple of bank notes.

Once the server walked away Finn asked, "What was all that about?"

"The young man over there speaks English. He may be able to tell us more about what's going on around here. You're best speaking to him, he'll notice my accent."

Finn hesitated, considered his options, then said, "Okay, I'll speak to him, wait here."

He walked across the diner and sat down next to the young man. Startled by the movement next to him the man looked up. Finn recognised the petrified look on his face, but before he could speak the man moved quickly to get off the bar stool as if trying to escape. His legs began to give way under the weight of his body but before he hit the floor, Finn grabbed his arm and pulled him back into the seat, "Steady lad, how many have you had?"

The young man's expression turned from one of panic and fear to surprise, "You're English?"

Finn looked around the bar and noticed a few customers beginning to look around at the sound of their voices, "Yes, but keep it down. The locals are starting to take an interest in us and we don't want to do that."

"Who are you? Are you from the mine? Have you come for me?"

Finn patted the young man on the back and lied, "Smith's the name. I'm a journalist from London. My boss thought it would be a good idea to send me to this hell hole to write an article on environmental issues related to mining. I'm struggling to find anyone who'll talk to me about the mines. The locals are wary of outsiders. What's your story? Why are you here?"

The young man mumbled, "Existence."

"You mean the environmental protection company? I hear it's just a group of climate activists into protesting. They won't like what's happening around here."

"They've taken over one of the old mines here. Up the mountain over the road, part of some experiment on green living."

"You're a climate activist?" Finn asked.

"Not really. Don't get me wrong I'm not happy about what's happening around the world but not like these guys.

187

They're hardcore. I'm a mechanical engineer. Existence was actively recruiting people from universities. That's where I first heard about them and after passing all the interviews, they offered me a job. The contract was to first help with setting the place up and then to take part in an experiment on sustainable living. It seemed like a good idea after finishing university in Auckland. A chance to do some travelling and to get some experience on my CV. I flew out here with a few of my university friends. We arrived among the first batches of contractors. I've been working inside the mine since the beginning. I'll be honest with you, the main reason I came here with my friends was the experiment at the end. The opportunity to spend two years with lots of young women. At the interview they told us that the project involved a fifty-fifty gender mix of similar age groups."

"What's happening in there now?" Finn asked.

"In the last week or so activity has increased. The refit is complete and now they're bringing in the final volunteers and supplies, hence all the delivery vans. They're getting ready to shut themselves inside."

Finn recognised the accent and changed the subject, "Auckland, you're a Kiwi far from home. What's your name buddy?"

"Jake Longford."

Finn held out a hand which was accepted, "Nice to meet you Jake. Why are you here? Are you allowed outside to socialise and get drunk? To be frank you look like you're in a bit of a mess. I noticed the look of panic on your face when I first spoke to you. What's the problem? I may be able to help."

Longford took a mouthful of beer before replying, "I got chucked out by the hard arsed bitch that runs the place. She was wandering around in a skin-tight black catsuit. It didn't leave much to the imagination. When she walked by, I did what most blokes would have done."

"What's that?"

"Told her she looked good."

"Yeah, I know what you mean. She had the same effect on me."

"You've met her?" Longford said with a surprised tone.

"Yesterday, she tried to terminate my contract also," Finn confirmed.

"Is that what happened to your face? Did you get a beating?"

"It's a long story but it sounds like we've both had a lucky escape,"

"She's a real hard bitch with an angel's face."

"Finish your story buddy. Why are you sitting here drinking by yourself?"

"Like I said she didn't like what I said and kicked me out of the place. I mean straight away, no chance for me to collect my gear or anything. Two guards took me outside and that's when I realised terminating my contract involved getting a bullet in the head. I managed to escape from the guards and have taken up refuge here. I've got no money or gear, I had to steal from a truck."

"What about the guards?"

"They followed me here but the locals chased them off. They don't like the environmentalists as they're campaigning to get the mines shut down."

"What's your plan now then?"

Longford looked at his near empty glass, shook it to stir up bubbles and said, "I've just spent my last few bucks on this beer then I'm going to start the task of hitchhiking to Stockholm."

"How'd you like to earn a free flight back to New Zealand?"

Longford's face changed to a smile, "You're joking, right?"

Finn shook his head, "You help me, and I'll help you."

"I'm interested for sure but it depends on what sort of help you need, I'm not into doing anything illegal."

Finn signalled to the bartender and ordered three beers. She placed them in front of the two men and walked away.

Finn stepped down from the bar stool and picked up two of the glasses, "If you're capable of walking, let's go over to my friend and talk about it."

Longford grabbed his pint, carefully stepped down from the bar stool and followed. Finn introduced Longford to Petrikov, sat down next to the Russian then gestured for the New Zealander to sit opposite.

Finn spoke, "Firstly, you're safe with us. We're going to our base in Gällivare tonight. If you come with us, talk to our people about the mine, then I promise that I'll drop you off at the local airport with enough money to get you home."

Longford looked cautiously at the two men and said, "Why do I get the feeling you're not really a journalist?"

"Your cat suited, angel faced, friend has stolen something from our bosses and they've sent us here to get it back. You're going to help us do that by telling us everything that's going on inside that mine. You can start by telling me how we get inside."

Longford went on to describe the layout, "There's only one way in and out, the front doors. Behind is a tunnel used as a storage area for vehicles then a decontamination chamber. Then you're inside the main facility, a large concourse area that splits into seven separate tunnels leading off in different directions, up, down, left, or right. It's like a rabbit's warren. Each tunnel leads to a larger chamber where they originally removed the iron ore. Some chambers are bigger than others, now they've been fitted out and designated for a particular usage."

Finn grabbed a napkin from the table and fumbled in his pocket for a pen. As Longford talked, he wrote notes and drew a map.

"The first tunnel is on the same level and has the living quarters. It's where they house all the people. Imagine a big hotel underground with rooms, canteen, recreation areas etc."

"Are each of the tunnels separated by doors?" Finn asked.

"Yes, each tunnel is self-sufficient with independent electrics, light, heat and ventilation."

"Tell me about the electric and air supply"

191

"There is a series of shafts, one for each tunnel, that serve various purposes. Fresh air intake, dirty air exhaust and an escape route in case of a problem in the mine like a collapse or something. A complex air scrubbing system monitors and controls the fresh air circulation. If the system detects any contamination in the outside fresh air it's cut off and the existing air in the mine has impurities removed by the scrubbers and recirculated. It means that you can live in the mine cut off from the outside world. The ventilation system also provides heating or cooling to maintain a temperature of twenty-one degrees. A bank of solar panels on the south side of the mountain provides a sustainable electricity source. If there are any problems with the solar panel supply there is a diesel backup generator in each tunnel. The air intake and exhaust for the generators is a sealed system, also piped out via the ventilation shafts. Each chamber can be cut off from the others leaving just the ventilation shaft escape hatch to get in or out."

"You just mentioned an escape hatch."

"Each shaft has a ladder up to a machine room that is linked to the maintenance room at the bottom. In the machine room there's a hatch to the outside but it can only be opened from inside using a digital code."

Finn gave up writing on the napkin which was now torn, "We're going to need you to tell our tech guys more about the shafts and how to get those hatches open. Once you've done that you can set off home. Okay?"

"How far is the place where the tech guys are based?"

"About an hour and a half from here."

"I'll just be happy to get as far away from this place as possible. But before we go…"

"Yes?" Finn enquired.

"How about another beer mate?"

❖ ❖ ❖ ❖

Finn and Petrikov carried Longford from the diner and threw him on the backseat of the Landcruiser. They climbed into the vehicle and began the drive back to the safehouse. The GPS application indicated they would arrive by seven o'clock. Finn mulled over what he had heard and considered his options. He pulled over on the grass verge, picked up the iBOW and quickly typed a message to Mac, *'Got some good intel...Back at 7. Get ready for a briefing when we return. Speak to Adams. Put the squad on alert'*

Finn put the iBOW down and began driving. He looked around at the sleeping man on the rear seat, "The guy is shattered, he's been living on his nerves the last couple of days."

Petrikov laughed, "He's also had one too many drinks…passing out is normally a sign."

"His knowledge of the mine is invaluable if we're to get in there and recover the stuff. It also sounds like our theory about her using it to prove a point was right. He's just confirmed that they're getting ready to lock themselves inside for a couple of years. To him it's just a bit of a joke, an opportunity to chase girls, but he's totally misunderstood the reality of the situation. This isn't a joke to her."

Petrikov announced, "The clue is in the name."

"How's that?" Finn invited, unsure of the Russian's comment.

"He said they call the place 'Början', that's Swedish for 'Beginning'. She's planning a new beginning for the world."

"Exactly, planning to wipe us all out in one big swipe and start again with a clean slate."

"Looks that way!"

Chapter 23
Början

Lars turned onto his side and looked at the digital clock. *05:47*.

He got up off the bed, collected his clothes from the floor, and rushed to the bathroom, taking care not to wake Bergqvist. He dressed, dampened down his hair with water from the sink then used a wristband to tie his hair into a ponytail. Leaving the room, he glanced at the naked body on the bed and wondered when he would get the chance again.

Arriving at the laboratory he found the chemist asleep at a desk, her head laid on a mess of papers. She awoke with a gasp when he barked, "Where's Molantra?"

She mumbled, "He's sleeping."

"There's no time for sleep. Fetch him immediately."

"No let him sleep. He's not slept for two days," she protested. She noticed the look on Lars's face change to one of rage then added, "He's completed the work that you've requested. The device is ready, he's even packed it up for you." She pointed to the corner of the room.

Lars followed her direction and noticed a large aluminium flight case with a smaller version on top. "Why two cases?" He asked.

"The large one is the device, the other holds the remote trigger."

Lars said excitedly, "Perfect! I'll collect it at noon. Make sure Molantra is here when I return. I want full training on how to operate the device.

❖ ❖ ❖ ❖

Bergqvist woke, happy to find that Lars had already left. She dressed in a green pair of trousers and a white t-shirt, both sustainably sourced from Pakistan. She slipped on a pair of shoes made from recycled materials and grabbed a coffee from the espresso machine.

She sat on the bed and switched on the TV. The news program presenter spoke of the latest global warming figures and estimated that by twenty fifty the world would be heading towards catastrophe. She smiled and spoke to the TV, "We'll already be well on the way to recovery by then."

She switched off the TV and threw the remote onto the bed. She used the telephone to request her Head of Security to join her. After several minutes there was a knock at the door and she let him into the room. Wallenberg entered, a large man, over six foot tall with long braided hair and beard, in his early forties with a scar on his left cheek. A memento from his days as a mercenary fighting in the jungles of Columbia.

A glint appeared in Bergqvist's eye that did not go unnoticed by him, "You wanted to see me boss?"

"Lars is leaving today with the weapon. He won't be returning, but keep that between us. We've agreed on a suitable target, Saint Petersburg, but it'll take him a few days to get the device set up. These are exciting times Wallenberg. We're finally moving to the next phase. Are your men ready?"

"Yes, everyone is ready. We're ready to stop anyone getting in or trying to get out. Can you now tell me the full details of the plan?"

"We'll shut ourselves in here and Lars will set off the device. Then I'll make a statement giving the leaders of the world two years to reverse the damage of climate change. If they refuse, we'll begin mass production of the biological agent and release it using the dispersion system."

"Is that what the group of engineers you asked me to dispose of were working on at the top of the mountain?"

"It's been designed to push the biological material into the lower atmosphere where it will spread all around the world. Afterwards we'll need to survive inside here for around fifty years. The mine has finished conversion into an independent and sustainable living system. But don't become complacent, once we shut the doors there'll be resistance from some of the occupants, they don't know the full details yet. Some will resist. Your job will be to eliminate that resistance immediately. If all goes to plan it'll be the children of our children that will enjoy the new world we create."

"All of the men are supportive of your cause, I personally selected them. No families or dependants and at the same time they all harbour a grudge against their relative governments for broken promises and lies. We'll do whatever you require boss," Wallenberg confirmed.

"There's another issue. Two men, a Russian and an Englishman, have been following me since I returned from Russia. They're determined to steal the biological material and I've got no doubt they'll soon turn up here. You need to tighten up base security and be prepared. Once Lars leaves with the device we'll close off the mine. There'll be no more access to the outside. Ensure all the vehicles and staff are inside, he'll be leaving here at thirteen hundred tomorrow."

Molantra ran through the operation of the device with Lars. It was easy enough, the complex electronics doing all the work. To communicate together the two parts of the weapon, the dispersion unit, and the trigger, needed activation by entering a code into the keypad on each part. The trigger was a modified satellite phone with a keypad, small display, and a button on the top protected by a cover.

Molantra explained that once the user established the communication link it was just a matter of flipping the safety cover off and pressing the button.

Despite the simplicity of the system Molantra became frustrated at repeating the process several times for the Swede to finally understand.

"Give me the codes again," Lars asked. Molantra gave up repeating the numbers and wrote them on a piece of paper instead.

Lars tested the number on the dispersion device, making it switch into the active state. While Lars played with the trigger the engineer quickly turned the dispersion device off again, just in case the Swede decided to test the trigger as well.

Lars stuffed the paper in his pocket, "Excellent."

He made a call and several maintenance staff appeared. They moved the flight cases to the outer storage area and loaded them into the red Range Rover Sport.

Molantra mumbled, "Now that we've completed the work…we'd both like to leave."

Lars smirked, "The work isn't complete. There's much more for you both to do."

"What work?" The chemist asked.

"We need you to start mass production of the biological substance, using the data and samples that we've provided."

"No! I won't do it. I want to leave straight away, that's what we agreed, my family needs me."

"Cast the thought from your mind, you'll both never see your families again."

Shocked by the statement the woman suddenly burst into tears, Molantra tried to grab Lars by the throat but before reaching him a security guard pushed him to the floor.

"I'll kill you," Molantra screamed.

Lars laughed then began walking away and at the airlock door he told a guard, "Throw them both in the brig. I'll deal with them later."

❖ ❖ ❖ ❖

In the vehicle storage area, Lars climbed into the Range Rover and rolled the window down.

Bergqvist leaned in and kissed him on the cheek, "Good luck my love."

She signalled to the security guard to open the mine entrance doors and he drove outside. In the rear-view mirror he observed Bergqvist and Wallenberg standing together as the doors closed behind him. He drove down the mountainside to the main road and set off on his journey to the port at Stockholm. The clock in the vehicle showed a time of 13:12.

With a fourteen-hour drive ahead of him, including a few food and petrol stops in between, he calculated his arrival to be sometime before dawn. With the weekly ferry sailing at 06.30 he had ample time to arrive safely. It would then just be a matter of clearing customs and joining the lines of vehicles waiting to board. He did not relish the thirty-eight hours stuck on board with tourists and lorry drivers. It would be a chore, boring and hopefully uneventful but once he was inside Russia he could push on with the mission. He felt pleased with himself, hopefully she would miss him while he was gone. Once he had proved his loyalty he could return and they would be together again.

❖ ❖ ❖ ❖

Wallenberg accompanied her to her room, "Do you need anything else boss?"

"Yes, there is something, come inside..."

She opened the door and he walked inside towards the middle of the room, hearing the door close and lock behind him. He turned to face her as she began removing her T-shirt revealing her naked breasts, "There's definitely something you can do for me."

Chapter 24
Briefing

Finn parked the Landcruiser and went to search for Strom, while Petrikov roused Longford who shouted out, "Where am I?"

"Our friend has brought you here to meet his buddies." Longford noticed the pistol handle sticking out of Petrikov's jacket and began struggling, unsure of what was happening to him.

Petrikov grabbed the young man's arms and said, "Relax! If we wanted to kill you, we'd have done it already. If you help us, we'll make sure you get that plane home."

Finn arrived with Strom who took Longford to a holding cell, but not before Finn explained the sensitive nature of the location and why it was best that he stayed locked up.

Longford accepted the situation, realising protesting would not improve things. Within ten minutes of Strom locking the door he was asleep on the small bed.

❖ ❖ ❖ ❖

Petrikov and Finn joined Mac and the others in the comms room.

"Okay, we're ready," Mac announced. "Tell us what you've found and why you've brought that young man with you."

Finn replied, "He's an engineer who's just had a run in with our lady mine owner. She wanted to permanently terminate his contract. Luckily, he met up with us before they stamped his card. He's been working inside there for the last couple of years doing all types of installation work. We've agreed to mutually help each other. He's given us a map of the layout of the mine including access points and security measures. We have nearly everything we could wish for. Once he sobers up you need to get the intelligence officers to debrief him. We need accurate information so we can formulate our plan."

"And what've you promised him in return?" Mac asked.

"A one-way, first-class ticket to Kiwi land. The least we can do for him."

"No problem. It won't make much difference if we don't get the biological weapon back," Mac said philosophically.

"Did you get in touch with Adams?" Finn asked.

"I did. He can get a team here tomorrow morning. But logistically I'm not sure how we get them into Sweden undetected."

"We can fly them into the local airport here, travelling in plain clothes on false papers. We've got everything that we need in the weapons store here but we'll need an extra couple of SUVs to get us to the mine."

Mac nodded, "I'll get Strom onto that straight away."

Finn turned to Petrikov, "I've got a figure in my head of how many men we'll need but I'd like to hear your thoughts first as you also heard what Longford had to say."

Petrikov shook his head in disapproval, "This is your mission Finn. I'll go along with whatever you decide. You're in charge."

Mac interrupted, "Technically I'm in charge but we won't split hairs."

Finn continued, "It's going to have to be a stealth mission. Any hint of a full-on assault will probably make her release the biological weapon. The large blast doors at the front are heavily guarded. The only vulnerable areas are the seven ventilation shafts which service each of the separate areas inside. They're scattered around the mountain side in concealed locations. My original idea was to use sleeping gas in all the air intakes but that won't work. Longford said the air scrubbers monitor the outside air and will lock the inlet and take over ventilation if there's any contamination. That means we must get inside. If we can get to the shafts undetected, we can use them to get inside. Each ventilation shaft has a hatch for maintenance and escape if required. To enter the hatch, we'll need to override the electronics and spring the deadbolts. Longford has given us details of what to expect once we get past the hatch. I'm thinking four, five-man, assault teams. Each team will be made up of four SAS soldiers and an IT guy."

"IT guy?" Mac asked.

"The whole mine is controlled by a complex electronics system that is managed from the server room. We need to secure the server and then we can lock down sections of the mine holding the staff inside the sectors until we secure the weapon. Each team will need an electronics expert who can first override the escape hatch lock then override other locks as required."

Finn looked around the table at the four intelligence officers, "That means you guys. So, make sure you obtain as much information from Longford on the functionality of the door locks including the software and electronics. If we can't get in, the whole mission will fail."

The four intelligence officers looked at each other nervously then looked at Mac who said, "Don't look at me, you all signed up to do whatever was required of you."

One spoke, "But we only have limited weapons training."

"If you need a weapon the mission has already failed and you'll probably all be dead anyway," Finn barked.

"You're all going. That's the last I want to hear of it." Mac growled.

Finn continued with his analysis, "We'll hit the four shafts closest to the laboratory. We can only assume that's where they've stored the biological material. According to Longford there are about forty security guards. Only security team members have clearance for the security sector so we don't know what arms they've got. What he's confirmed is that he's only ever seen the security guards carrying assault rifles and pistols. Once we get inside, we'll split into teams, each with a specific goal, to secure a sector. In simple terms what we need to do is neutralise the guards, secure the biological weapon, lockdown the employees and secure the facility."

Finn looked to the intelligence officers, "Do you have a satellite image of the mine? Longford said to gain access to the ventilation shafts, they constructed a maintenance road on the mountainside that is hidden from the main road."

One officer spoke up, "I will print it off for you."

The officer collected the large A3 image from the printer and laid it on the table in front of Finn and the others. It clearly showed the tarmac road, truck stop and the dirt track leading to the main entrance. Using the tarmac road as a reference Finn followed it beyond the truck stop, searching for the maintenance road Longford had mentioned.

He pointed at the image, "There! Look you can just make out a track through the trees."

He followed the road with his finger. As the maintenance road weaved up the side of the mountain it split many times, with separate tracks heading off in other directions. Finn imagined where the tunnels would be located under the mountain and began picking out the locations of the ventilation shafts at the ends of the tracks, circling each one with a felt pen. He picked up the sketch that Longford had given him and compared it against the satellite image. On the top of each shaft, he wrote a name - archive, store, biosphere, accommodation, IT, security, research. He returned to the main track and continued following its path. It stopped at the top of the mountain where there was a larger concrete structure with a series of large pipes pointing upwards.

"What's this thing? It looks like a set of chimneys. Longford didn't mention anything on the top of the mountain. Wait here."

Finn grabbed the satellite image and rushed to the holding cell. He woke Longford and showed him the satellite image, "Do you know what that is?"

"No. They wouldn't let anyone go up there. A separate group of engineers and builders started building it about eight months ago. They didn't mix with the other contractors, then one day they just disappeared. I guessed that the contract had finished so thought no more about it."

"They look like chimneys of some kind?"

"I don't think so, there's nothing in the mine that needs to be burnt, everything is recycled. All I know is that it's got something to do with the research sector. There's a room in there that no one can enter without authorisation."

Finn locked the holding cell and returned to the briefing room, "He doesn't know what it is but it must be important as its connected to the research area and no doubt somehow to the weapon."

The men all looked at each other, thinking the same thing but daring not to say what it was.

Finn picked up a pen, wrote down a list of names on a scrap of paper and passed it to Mac, "Get these guys here by tomorrow morning."

Mac read the list then said, "There's a name missing."

The response shocked Finn, "How's that?"

"My name's not there."

"What?"

"I'm coming with you. Don't worry you're still in charge of the mission but I can lead a team. I know my stuff and I'm just as anxious as you to get that biological material into safe hands."

Finn reached out and took the paper, he quickly scribbled out a name and handed it back, "You're in."

The next morning the guys arrived in groups on alternate flights from Oslo and Stockholm. The first group flying in from Oslo landed at 07:23, dressed in civilian clothes like the transient miners who regularly passed through the area. The border control guard skimmed over the immigration documents then ushered them through to the exit where Strom was waiting with the transit van.

The first group included Corporal Gray, Rowntree, Docherty, and Nolan. Strom showed them to a room where they quickly dumped their gear. Their orders were to remain in the living room until the other members of the assault force arrived.

O'Neill, Jones, Herd and Ford arrived on the next flight from Stockholm at 08:23. The final flight from Oslo arrived at 10:48 with Borthwick, Currie, Heaney, Pallin and Hind.

The lounge grew noisy as the men arrived and broke off into smaller groups, keeping themselves occupied and eating food and drinking coffee. The main group took up station on and around the sofa, watching the TV. Unable to understand the language they swapped sexist remarks about the female TV presenters instead.

Finn, Petrikov and Mac kept themselves out of the way in the comms room downstairs until ready to address the men.

Finn spoke up, "What about the extra vehicles?"

Mac replied, "Strom has managed to get hold of two Fermel Maverick LDVs that are used quite a bit over here in the mining industry. They're second hand, battered and bruised, reliable and built like a tank. I'm not sure how he did it, but it's best not to ask. They're getting dropped off in the next hour."

"Sounds perfect."

"They'll blend in as well as a bikini on Miami Beach," Mac joked.

"How many seats?"

"The Trooper model holds up to twelve men, the other, a Dual Cab, takes four. With the Landcruiser that gives us enough space to get everyone and the gear to site."

Finn nodded then announced, "Let's go and tell the men why they're here."

The three men ventured upstairs into the main room. Finn turned the TV off and waited until the protests had died down before speaking, "You'll be wondering why you've been dragged out to the Swedish wilderness at short notice. And it'll come as no surprise to you if I answer that question by saying that we've been given a job that no one else is crazy enough to take on."

The men cheered and clapped.

Rowntree shouted from his perch on the arm of the sofa, "Any chance of meeting any Swedish women on this mission boss?"

More cheers and whistles applauded the question.

Finn grinned, "Actually, yes!" The men continued with their frivolity until Finn declared, "Okay, settle down guys, time to talk about the mission."

Finn called Mac and Petrikov over to stand alongside him in front of the TV. He heard some muttering at the rear of the room, the usual barrack room humour. Ignoring the comments, he proceeded to introduce the two men, "This handsome chap is Major Petrikov. He's feeling a little bit delicate as you can see. The name may give you a hint that he's from Russian military intelligence."

Some of the men began whispering while others stared intensely at the Russian, remembering days when the two forces had crossed paths.

Petrikov held up his hands in submission, "Don't worry guys, I'm only here for the vodka."

O'Neill shouted out, "Save me some."

Petrikov opened his mouth to respond but was cut off by Finn "And this gentleman is Mac. He's from MI6, but don't let that put you off, he used to be a Bootneck."

Whistles and catcalls broke out around the room.

Corporal Jones quipped, "Is your suit in the wash?"

Above the laughter Mac said, "I'm here just in case you guys get into bother and need some help getting the job finished."

Finn patted the MI6 agent on the back, "Now that the introductions are over let's get down to business. There's a converted mine seventy or so miles north of here that's occupied by a group of climate activists. The leader of this group is a Swedish woman called Agneta Bergqvist. We believe she's in possession of a biological weapon that she stole from a Russian research facility. Only a small number of people at the highest levels of British government knew about the theft. Mac has been on the case from the start. He brought in the Major and myself to track the weapon down. The Prime Minister has just informed his Swedish counterpart about our mission. The Swedes are not happy but have agreed, for now, to avoid public panic and the news getting out, we should continue with our plan. We suspect that Bergqvist is going to set off this biological weapon, possibly in a major European city. We're confident that the biological weapon is still in the mine and they've not implemented their plan."

Finn stopped talking and looked around the room, the soldiers stared back, each one processing the information he'd relayed to them. Seeing that he had their full attention he said forcefully, "Gentlemen the task is clear, we're going to break into the mine and secure that weapon."

"What's this biological weapon boss? And how did this woman get hold of it?" Docherty shouted out from the side of the room.

211

"That information is classified," Mac said firmly.

Finn replied, "All you need to know Doc is that if it's activated then everyone on site and the surrounding area will be killed. No survivors."

The room went silent, the seriousness of the mission now sinking in. Finn noticed the faces of the men in front of him change from relaxed to the intense, battle ready, state that he recognised. A look that he knew he could depend upon.

He let the information sink in for a few more moments before continuing, "We've got no firm intel on the strength of resistance that we may come up against, the last estimate was forty or so guys. An informer who has worked there for the last two years has given us a layout of the mine. He's also told us that the security guards remind him of the special forces guys he's seen on TV. We'll have to assume they're probably ex-Swedish military or possibly mercenaries. Regardless of where they're from you can be sure that they'll be highly trained and motivated. We need to be ready for a high level of resistance."

Corporal Gray asked, "What's the plan boss?"

Finn replied, "Good question. This is how we're going to do it…"

Finn went on to explain the full details of the assault plan that he had formulated with Mac and Petrikov.

❖ ❖ ❖ ❖

"These are the squads." Finn pulled out a scrap of paper

from his pocket. "Alpha squad will be led by myself with O'Neill, Currie and Heaney. Major Petrikov will lead Bravo squad along with Rowntree, Ford and Borthwick. Mac will lead Charlie team with Corporal Jones, Nolan and Pallin. The last squad will be led by Corporal Gray with the remaining rabble, Docherty, Herd and Hind."

Finn pointed to the four MI6 intelligence officers standing at the rear of the room, "Each squad will have an IT guy as support. Their job is to circumvent the security system and unlock the ventilation shaft escape hatch. They'll also help by overriding the electronics in the tunnels. By taking control of the server room, we can use the modern electronic systems to our advantage by overriding and locking the doors in the tunnels. That way we can keep the staff locked down in each sector."

The SAS soldiers looked around at the intelligence men standing behind them. Their faces gave the game away. Rowntree shouted, "They look petrified."

A few laughs fluttered around the room, Docherty added, "Don't worry guys we'll make sure you get home in one piece."

Finn continued, "Just make sure you do. Without them the mission will fail."

He let his comments sink in then added, "Mac's squad will secure the computer server in tunnel five. Petrikov's squad will deal with the main security team that is based in tunnel six. Corporal Gray will secure the accommodation block in tunnel four. I'm going after the biological weapon in tunnel seven. As all the tunnels merge into a central concourse we'll all need to secure tunnels one to three if the IT guy in the server room cannot lock them down."

He looked at his watch, "We leave here at twenty-two hundred hours. That gives you just over an hour to get your shit together. Write your letters and give them to Strom when you pick up your uniforms. We may be working undercover but we're not spies. Carry your berets and make sure your union jack badge is on your tunic. We are travelling in civilian vehicles posing as mine workers so coats over your uniform's gentlemen. We'll discard them when we start the attack. We're going in as British soldiers. We're going to be hooked up to the usual squad comms system but keep radio chatter to a minimum."

Hind held his hand up, Finn pointed at him to speak, "What about weapons boss?"

Finn smiled, "Strom has a room full of them downstairs. Remember this place is a converted mine made up of lots of tunnels and rooms. We're going in light so it's close combat gear only, assault rifles, pistols, knives, smoke grenades and flashbangs. You're going to have to quickly identify, and separate, the innocent civilians from the terrorists and guards."

Finn paused and looked around at the men waiting for another question, or comment, but none came. The silence told him the men had begun mentally preparing for the mission. Upon deaf ears he announced, "Dismissed!"

Chapter 25
Operation Örn

The three vehicles left the safehouse on time at 22:02. Finn led the way, driving his squad in the Landcruiser. Petrikov, driving the Dual Cab, and his squad followed. The remaining guys climbed into the Trooper with Mac at the wheel.

The journey was uneventful. At the Truckstop Finn passed the mine entrance road and continued for another five hundred yards until he spotted the maintenance road. The entrance to the dirt road had large gates covered in camouflage netting which blended in with the vegetation. To anyone driving along the tarmac road it would have been practically invisible.

Finn pulled the vehicle onto the grass verge with the others stopping behind. He signalled to O'Neill in the passenger seat who quickly climbed out, ran over to the gates, and broke the lock with a heavy-duty bolt cutter. He swung the large gates open to let the convoy drive inside, then closed the gates and secured them with tie-wraps.

The vehicles parked on the dirt road, hidden from the main road and Finn gathered the squad leaders together. They synchronised watches and agreed to launch the assault at zero two hundred hours, a time when most of the inhabitants would be sleeping and caught off guard. It also allowed each squad over two hours to find their allocated ventilation shaft, disable any security measures and overcome the electronics on the escape hatch lock. They wished each other luck, climbed into their vehicles, and continued up the mountain road.

Finn found the dirt road to be in surprisingly good condition, a sign of the amount of work that had taken place converting the mine. He kept the Landcruiser in low gear, following the contours of the mountainside and slowing on several sharp bends. The vertical drop on the side of the road generated some concern but he pushed on regardless. Halfway up the mountainside he came to the first junction with a road that headed downwards in the direction of the front of the mine then disappearing into the trees. He drove past the junction, stopped then looked in his wing mirror seeing Mac take the new track. As agreed, Mac would drop off Corporal Gray and his team for shaft four then continue to shaft five. At the next junction he stopped and watched as Petrikov headed down the track towards ventilation shaft six.

Finn continued to the next junction, left the main track, and followed the new route to shaft seven. The track suddenly stopped and he parked the Landcruiser, "This is as far as we go."

He climbed out alongside O'Neill, Heaney, Currie, and the intelligence officer. The men took up defensive positions as he surveyed the area. Where the road stopped there was a large metal cage, painted green to blend in with the surrounding vegetation. The cage was on the perimeter of a twenty-foot square concrete pad. A series of pipes stuck upwards from the flat surface along with a five-foot-wide square metal fan grille and a metal hatch. The cage had a single padlocked gate and, in the corner, a single security camera pointing down towards the hatch. A series of cables ran down from the gate to a junction box. *Alarm.*

He signalled to O'Neill, pointing out the camera position and alarm mechanism.

O'Neill nodded, took out the bolt cutters and cut a hole in the fence below the camera. He moved inside the cage ensuring to stay out of the camera view. From below he gently bent the camera upwards towards the top of the cage. A quick fix which would hopefully allow them to enter undetected because cutting the camera feed would set off the alarm inside the security room. All they had to hope now was that the camera operator was half asleep. Once he had completed his work, he signalled the others and they entered through the hole in the cage.

Finn looked at his watch, *00:36.*

The intelligence officer busied himself working on the electronics. Using a digital meter, he scanned the area around the hatch and located the keypad on the other side, marking the spot with a chalk mark. He took out a larger piece of equipment, a magnetic scanner and placed it over the chalk mark. Taking out a bolt gun he fired bolts through the bracket of the scanner into the concrete. He checked that the scanner was secure then opened a laptop screen from the top, revealing a keyboard.

The officer began typing into the keyboard and an image appeared on the screen. Faint green lines showing the size, shape and wiring in the keypad on the other side.

He started a software program and watched as the magnetic scanner began reading the small electrical pulses controlling the hatch locks. A digital readout on the laptop screen began to fill up with numbers. Once the last of the eight numbers required to open the lock appeared, he looked at Finn who gave him a thumbs up. The officer pressed the enter key on the keyboard and the deadlocks on the escape hatch disengaged.

Finn pressed the comms button on his neck, "Alpha ready."

He stared at the hatch. *Now we wait.*

Each of the teams had to overcome the same security measures and unlock the hatch mechanism, gradually each one of them called in.

At 01:17 Petrikov at shaft six called, "Bravo ready."

At 01:36 Mac at shaft five called, "Charlie ready."

The teams called based on how far they had to travel to reach their designated shaft. Corporal Gray, at shaft four, was the furthest away, the accommodation sector, central to the mine layout.

The other teams waited patiently until Gray called at 01:47, "Delta ready"

Finn's team readied themselves. He stared at the digital counter on his watch, urging the numbers to scroll forward.

At 02:00 Finn pressed the comms button and announced, "Operation Örn, go."

With help from O'Neill, he grabbed the handles on the hatch and heaved the heavy steel door open until it lay the concrete. He peered into the machine room below making sure it was empty, jumped down and stepped to the side while the rest of the squad joined him. The roar of the five-foot-wide fan unit made talking impossible.

He opened the internal hatch, revealing a ladder leading down into the mine. At the very bottom he could see a darkened void, the maintenance room that Longford had described. He estimated the ladder was at least two hundred feet long. He climbed onto the ladder and made quick work getting down to the bottom in a matter of minutes by using a technique that he'd seen sailors do by jumping several rungs at a time while holding onto the ladder sides with his hands. The team followed and regrouped at the bottom in the darkened room.

Finn found a light switch on the wall. The sudden burst of white light revealed the layout of the maintenance room. A collection of tubes, pipes and cables ran along the ceiling. Standing in the corner, two large diesel generators connected to banks of fuse boxes and control panels along the wall. He tried the door handle, *Locked.*

The IT guy plugged a small handheld device into a network port on the wall and after a few moments the lock opened.

Finn turned off the room light then slowly opened the door, seeing bright lights on the other side. He waited for his eyes to adjust to the brightness then opened the door wider into a corridor flanked on both sides by white partitions, half glass to the ceiling. Each of the partitioned rooms had various chemical warning signs on the doors and windows. The corridor was about sixty feet long and

219

at the end it opened into a bigger room, white and clinical looking. In the distance he noticed some unarmed, white coated, figures moving around. *Workers.*

❖ ❖ ❖ ❖

Delta team with Corporal Gray, Docherty, Herd, Hind with an IT guy in support had the hardest task, securing the accommodation area. While waiting for the go ahead, Gray showed his team the layout drawing which Longford had given him.

It showed the ventilation shaft door located at a mid-point in the structure, entering directly onto a central atrium. To the right of the atrium the main living quarters constructed on two levels. Rooms which, for most of the inhabitants, were small, designed with a dual-purpose shower and toilet cubicle and space for two bunk beds. Despite the rooms having modern features and furniture they still resembled an upmarket prison cell.

The recreational areas were to the left of the atrium and included a spa, gym, lounge area, swimming pool, and a large room for team sports such as football and basketball. Beyond the recreational areas there was a smaller atrium leading on to some higher spec living quarters used by the management, including Bergqvist. These led to the sector access door. As with all the tunnels there was a decontamination chamber at the access door that once locked isolated each tunnel. Once clear of the decontamination chamber it would mean a short hike up tunnel four to the main concourse of the mine.

Gray spoke to his squad, "Guys this isn't going to be easy, we've got a lot of people to very quickly take control of. If Longford is right there'll also be several security staff to contend with. Our goal is to get to the sector access tunnel as quickly as possible without killing any civilians. Any fucker who points a gun at you is a terrorist and those guys you can kill. Once past the decontamination chamber, with the help of our IT friend here, we'll be able to shut off the whole sector and seal all the civilians inside. Understood?"

The squad nodded in agreement.

Docherty said, "Corp, can I suggest we do it like a bank robbery. Smoke the area then go in loud and lively. That should catch the people, who are not in bed sleeping, off guard. We get them down on the ground and that'll highlight the guards so we can deal with them. Once everyone is on the ground and the guards are neutralised, we make a dash for the access door."

"I Agree, good plan Doc," Gray confirmed. He turned to the IT guy, "You stay behind us. Only use the pistol if you need to."

When the 'Go' signal came from Finn they quickly made their way down to the maintenance room at the bottom of the ladder. They stood patiently while the IT guy did his electronic magic trick and unlocked the door. Gray and Docherty took out a flashbang each, the others held smoke grenades. Gray slowly opened the door a fraction and looked out into the atrium, seeing only a handful of people milling around. He spotted a security guard on the upper landing carrying an assault rifle and another in the main atrium near the information desk.

Using hand signals he indicated the danger to the others. On a count of three he kicked open the door and they each threw in the grenades. The flashbangs disorientated the people moving around, the smoke completed the task. Gray ran out into the atrium shouting, "Everyone on the ground now."

Docherty followed, in time to spot the guard on the first-floor landing aiming his weapon at Gray. He quickly raised his own assault rifle and shot the guard with three rounds into the chest. The guard flopped forward, rotated on the guard rail, and fell onto the atrium floor.

The flashbang that landed at the feet of the guard near the information desk generated temporary blindness. Gray took the opportunity to run towards him, knocking him out cold with the butt of his rifle.

The smoke, explosions and shooting brought about panic in the remaining civilians. Most people began running in the direction of the access tunnel. Hind and Herd ran towards it shooting rounds above the people's heads and began repeating the order to get down onto the floor. The vast majority complied. Gray showed the handful of belligerent ones the error of their ways by shoving them down to the floor.

Docherty began moving backwards until he joined Hind and Herd, the IT guy by his side. Gray fired more shots into the air and joined the others at the entrance to a corridor lined on either side with the doors into the recreational areas. People began coming out of the rooms, confused by all the noise. Gray and Herd forced the civilians back into the sports rooms as they progressed along the corridor.

Docherty and Hind remained on guard to block anyone from the atrium trying to get into the recreation corridor. A security guard appeared from a room on the far end of the atrium, firing an assault rifle.

The bullets hit the wall and ricocheted around Docherty's head. He ducked, grabbed the IT guy, who had frozen to the spot, pushed him into the corridor behind and shouted, "Have you got a death wish laddie? Stay there and keep your bloody head down."

Hind returned fire while bullets rained around him and a piece of shrapnel cut into the side of his face. Docherty crouched down, fired off three shots and the guard collapsed in a heap. He looked at Hind, blood running down his face and said, "You're hit."

Hind replied, "Don't worry, I'm still breathing."

Gray and Herd arrived at the far end of the recreation corridor, finding another smaller atrium with a change of decor. He realised they'd reached the high specification living quarters. On the opposite side of the small atrium there was another corridor, with a collection of four rooms, two on each side. Looking further beyond the small corridor he found the goal, the sector access door.

A door suddenly opened on the left side and a blonde woman, dressed all in black, ran out into the corridor wildly shooting an assault rifle. Bullets travelled across the small atrium to where the two SAS soldiers were standing and ricocheted all around the corridor.

Herd took a direct hit in the centre of his chest. The force of the bullet knocked him onto his back while the bullet proof vest saved his life.

Gray reacted immediately and returned fire as the blonde woman threw a flashbang into the atrium. He spotted it approaching and quickly closed his eyes. The force of the blast drove him, stumbling, backwards into the recreation corridor.

Docherty observed what was happening and began running up from the other end of the recreation corridor. Hind and the IT guy followed. He grabbed Gray, pulling him out of the way and started shooting back towards the woman's last position.

As the smoke cleared there was no sign of her. Herd gathered his breath and began getting to his feet, helped by the IT guy.

Gray opened his eyes and shouted, "Who was that mad bitch?"

Docherty quipped, "It's a good job she's a lousy shot."

They regrouped, headed across the mini atrium and into the small corridor. After passing through the decontamination chamber, they came out into a large rock faced tunnel. In the distance, a hundred feet away they could see the main concourse at the entrance to the mine.

The blonde-haired woman was barking orders at people then disappeared to the left.

The IT guy worked feverishly at the electronics on the door lock, trying to override the computer control.

A group of six security guards appeared at the far end of the tunnel and ran towards them, shooting assault rifles. The SAS soldiers returned fire but with no cover available in the tunnel. Two guards fell immediately, the others continued advancing. The IT guy cried out in pain as a bullet pierced his arm.

Docherty shouted, "Bollocks to this turkey shoot, come on, let's get these fuckers."

He set off with Hind alongside, running towards the guards and firing off bullets in short accurate bursts. Two more guards fell. The remaining two, seeing their comrades fall, lost their appetite for a fight, dropped their weapons, and surrendered.

Hind and Docherty ran up to the guards, knocked them onto the ground, tied their arms behind their backs and dragged them over to the rock wall.

Gray checked on the IT guy, "Is the door locked."

Gripping the wound on his arm, between gasps of pain, the IT guy mumbled, "Yes."

Gray checked the wound, "You'll live, and you've also got a story to impress the women down the pub with." He signalled to Hind who helped the IT guy to his feet.

Delta team regrouped and progressed down the tunnel towards the main concourse. In the distance they could hear shooting and grenades exploding, all from the actions of the other assault teams.

Taking up a defensive position at the end of the tunnel Gray pressed his comms button and reported, "Delta team, accommodation block secure, one injured, seven guards down, two captured."

❖ ❖ ❖ ❖

Mac and his squad of Corporal Jones, Nolan, Pallin and IT guy entered via shaft five escape hatch, without any issues. They made their way down the ladder to the maintenance room, where the noise from the equipment made talk impossible due to the stocks of additional air conditioning units needed to maintain a steady temperature of fourteen degrees centigrade in the server room.

Unfortunately, Longford was unable to supply details of the layout of the IT sector. All he could say was that it had a heavily guarded entrance with only authorised personnel allowed access. The squad had to assume that the interior would have a similar layout to the other tunnels. A fitted-out chamber leading to an airlock, the outer tunnel, and the main concourse. The squad's goal was to secure the server room, eliminate any resistance and lockdown any staff working there.

The IT worked on the door security and unlocked it. Mac drew a pistol, and slowly opened the door into the server room. The other members of the squad stood patiently behind him ready to respond to whatever would greet them.

Mac opened the door into a large void containing racks of computer hard drives set out in rows. The brain of Början, the system that controlled everything in the facility, from monitoring heat, light, air quality and security, down to watering the plants in the biosphere and setting the mood lighting in the recreation area. Without a brain the facility would descend into chaos and the small assault team would lose control.

Mac adopted a crouched position and moved from the doorway into the room and over to one of the rows. At the far end of the row to himself, he noticed a couple of engineers working at computer terminals and the airlock door in the distance. He signalled to the others to join him and they quickly took up defensive positions behind him.

The IT guy plugged a laptop into a network point and started typing. The SAS soldiers watched as the two men working at the computer terminals became animated. One shouted something, then ran over to the other. Together they stared at a monitor then one slammed his hand down on a panel. A loud alarm suddenly rang out and orange flashing lights on the ceiling illuminated the area.

The IT guy said nervously, "They've detected me accessing the system."

Mac changed the magazine in his pistol to tranquiliser rounds and moved along the row of hard drives towards the men. From the end of the rack, he shot two darts in quick succession. The first hit one of the computer

227

operators on the neck, causing him to flinch in reflex. Seconds later the man was slumped down on the floor. The other operator looked in horror then felt a sharp pain in his own chest and joined his friend.

The squad's IT guy continued to work feverishly on the laptop. Corporal Jones turned to him and barked, "For fucks sake mate can you shut that bloody alarm off?"

Also exasperated the IT guy replied, "I'm trying."

"Well try harder," Jones added.

The airlock door opened and six security guards rushed into the server room, taking the SAS soldiers off guard. The security guards split up and took up defensive positions behind desks and various computer cabinets.

Mac shouted, "Spread out, find cover."

The men did as he ordered.

Jones ran to the far end of the server racks and over to the outer wall. He crouched down and edged along the wall until he was level with the end of the racks. Further along the rows he noticed Mac crouched down, fumbling with the magazine in his pistol.

A burst of bullets ripped along the plastic cladding above Jones's head and he dived onto the floor. Rolling onto his back he fumbled in his harness and found a flashbang. Almost instantly he pulled the pin and threw it in the direction of the shooting. The grenade went off with a loud noise and a flash of bright white light, temporarily blinding the two guards behind a desk. Confused, one stood up and stumbled forward. Jones used his pistol to eliminate him then crawled along the floor towards the desk. While the other squad members had their own battles to his right, he waited. The second guard's sight began to return and he took the reckless decision to look over the edge of the desk. Jones reached up, grabbed the guard's neck and with his other hand drove a hunting knife under the man's jaw into his brain. A stream of blood squirted out over Jones's face and tunic. The guard's body jerked as his brain sent out the final electrical signals, then he slumped down to the floor.

From behind the desk Jones observed a group of guards hiding on Mac's side of the room. Nolan moved a few rows down from where Mac had taken up station and proceeded to the end of the rack. Jones spotted Nolan appear, seeing the danger, he shouted a warning but a hail of bullets drowned out the sound as they tore into Nolan's body. Mac gave up on the jammed pistol and threw it away. He swung the assault rifle from his back and shot at the guard who was shooting towards Nolan. In some strange synchronised death dance both the guard and Nolan collapsed to the floor.

The other guards returned fire at Mac and he pressed his body against the computer rack to avoid the bullets. The IT guy dropped the laptop and cowered in the corner as bullets ripped into the computer hard drives around him.

Pallin moved forward alongside Mac, the pair looked left to the prone body of Nolan in the next row. Jones, to their right, on the other side of the room, caught their attention by waving. The three SAS soldiers began signalling each other, formulating a plan to overpower the guards.

Mac and Pallin threw flashbangs towards the three remaining guards. The detonation of the flashbangs forced them to stop shooting and seek cover instead. While the guards hid, Jones took the opportunity to proceed further along the wall towards the airlock door behind the guards. Mac and Pallin grabbed the chance to advance, taking up cover behind a large desk.

Jones used his assault rifle to cut down the nearest guard. The other two looked around, startled to see Jones. Realising they were moments from death they threw down their weapons and stepped forward with hands held high. Pallin and Jones advanced, hit them both in the face with their rifle butts, knocking them out cold. They turned the limp bodies over and tie wrapped their hands behind their backs.

Mac moved to the IT guy, "Stop messing about and get on with it. We've got to take control of the system."

The IT guy picked up the computer and continued hacking into the system.

Mac ran towards the airlock door, shouting at the others as he ran, "Jones, come with me, we need to support the others in the main concourse. Pallin, look after the IT guy. Make sure he locks down sections one to three or we'll have people roaming around everywhere."

Mac pressed his comms button and reported the squad's progress to the others, "Charlie team, IT block secure, one dead, four guards down, two captured."

Mac and Jones passed through the airlock into the stone walled tunnel and headed towards the main concourse, assault rifles at the ready.

❖ ❖ ❖ ❖

Bergqvist ran from the accommodation section into the main concourse. A group of security guards appeared and she shouted, "We've got intruders in the accommodation block, get there now."

The guards ran off towards tunnel four and an ultimate showdown with Corporal Gray and his men.

She tried to access the security sector in tunnel six but changed her mind when she heard shooting, Petrikov's group meeting resistance from the guards inside. She cursed then ran towards the research tunnel.

❖ ❖ ❖ ❖

Petrikov's team gathered in the maintenance room attached to the security sector below shaft six. A guard on the other side suddenly opened the door just as the IT guy began to override the lock mechanism. The IT guy and the guard stared at each other for a moment before the Russian grabbed the man's jacket and pulled him inside the room. Rowntree hit the guard in the face with the butt of his assault rifle and he collapsed unconscious. Ford quickly tie-wrapped his hands behind his back and dragged him into the corner.

Hearing the noise another guard approached the door, spotted the men, and shouted out, "Intruders!"

The four soldiers took up positions around the doorway, two crouching on one knee with the others standing behind. Petrikov shot the approaching guard with a burst of bullets and he fell in a heap. He took a moment to quickly survey the area outside the maintenance room which he discovered was at the rear of the room. He spotted the airlock door at the far end, to the left a row of bunk beds, on the right a series of rooms. He read the signs on the doors. The closest read *Brig*, followed by *Toilets*, *Showers*, *Armoury*, *Canteen, Office* and at the far end *Security Chief*. He counted the guards that had taken up positions around the room, hiding behind beds, furniture and in the doorways of some of the rooms.

Bullets began to pepper the walls around the maintenance room doorway and the four soldiers returned inside to take cover. Petrikov and Borthwick pulled flashbangs from their harnesses and threw them into the room. The guards nearest to them became disoriented by the flashbangs. Petrikov and Borthwick shot blindly into the smoke, aiming at where the guards had been located. As the smoke cleared, they noticed two dead guards and three more on the floor seriously injured, rolling around in pain as they slowly died.

A guard headed for the *Armoury* door, trying to get supplies. Petrikov observed the movement and shot, forcing him back under cover.

Rowntree shouted, "Let's smoke the bastards out."

The four soldiers pulled out a combination of smoke and flashbang grenades. On a count of three they threw two each into the void, aiming at different parts of the room. They hid in the maintenance room, while the explosions rang out. Petrikov moved left out of the doorway, firing at the shapes moving around in the smoke. Rowntree moved right doing the same. Borthwick and Ford standing together in the doorway, fired rounds towards the other end of the room. Petrikov hid behind a bunk bed and quickly reloaded. Rowntree reached the toilet door, kicked it open and took up cover at the doorway. The smoke cleared and the number of bodies lying on the floor had increased.

After a slight lull in the action the *Security Chief* door suddenly burst open. A large man appeared in the doorway, holding a M249 machine gun at chest level. The man shouted something in Swedish and began firing wildly. Armour piercing tracer bullets ricocheted all around the maintenance room doorway.

The ferocity of the onslaught caught Ford off guard as he took bullets across his body. One hit him in the neck which tore his carotid artery in two. He clasped his hand to the wound, blood flooded out around his fingers as he fell to the floor, already dead.

Borthwick took hits on his left leg and arm. The force of the bullets spun his body around and he fell back into the maintenance room. The IT guy, hiding behind a generator, ran over, grabbed Borthwick under the armpits and dragged his body further into the room, and safety.

Petrikov recognised the danger the large calibre machine gun posed and quickly threw a frag grenade towards the shooter.

Seeing the grenade approaching, the shooter ran away from the office door towards the airlock and the remaining six guards joined him. The grenade blast destroyed the office door and started a fire.

The man shouted, "Retreat!" pressed a button on the airlock and disappeared inside with the guards.

Petrikov and Rowntree ran to the airlock, seeing the guards disappearing out of the other side into the rock faced tunnel. As the room began to fill with smoke, they returned to the maintenance room and collected Borthwick, the IT guy and Ford's body. As they ran towards the airlock the sprinkler system activated covering them in cold water. The water quickly extinguished the flames and a mixture of smoke and steam filled the room.

At the airlock door the IT guy desperately tried to override the lock. After a few tries the lock disengaged, allowing them to proceed into the airlock. They exited out the other side in time to see the man with the M249 standing at the far end of the tunnel talking to a woman. The two began shouting orders at the guards then disappeared to the left.

Petrikov barked, "Rowntree, come with me." He turned to the IT guy, pointed to Borthwick, and added, "You look after him."

The Russian and Rowntree reloaded, taking extra magazines and grenades from Borthwick's harness, before setting off towards the concourse. The six guards found cover and started firing in short bursts, trying to pick the two men off.

Petrikov moved to the left tunnel wall, Rowntree moved right. Petrikov found a space in the rock face giving sufficient cover for him to be able to return fire while Rowntree did the same on the other side. Progress was slow, under constant fire from the guards.

In an unbelievable partnership the SAS soldier and Russian GRU officer made gradual progress up the tunnel, taking turns to shoot, then moving forward, covering each other as they progressed. As they got closer to the guards, they ran out of hiding spaces and stopped the advance.

The two soldiers looked at each other and considered their options. Bullets rang out from the right of the concourse, two guards fell, another turned to return fire then collapsed dead, the remaining three surrendered.

Petrikov and Rowntree came out into the tunnel and walked forward, guns still drawn. From the right in the main concourse Mac and Jones appeared and quickly tie-wrapped the hands of the surrendered guards.

Rowntree regrouped with the other SAS soldiers rounding up civilians in the concourse while Mac and Petrikov headed towards the research tunnel.

❖ ❖ ❖ ❖

Finn continued to review the area outside the research sector maintenance room door. No guards appeared which allowed him the freedom to move into the corridor and investigate the first partitioned room. A typical laboratory, empty of people but packed with clinical and medical equipment. He signalled to O'Neill to join him and together they moved along the corridor taking a side each, finding all the labs unoccupied. The electronic lock on each laboratory door required entry of a code into a keypad on the side before it could open.

At the end of the corridor, they stopped their advance, seeing people working at a workstation counter in a large white panelled room, a man and woman. Along the right side of the room there was a much larger laboratory with a partition almost made entirely from glass. Beyond, on the far wall of the white room he could see the entrance to the airlock door.

Finn tapped on the glass partition next to him and the workers looked up. Finn showed his pistol and gestured for the two workers to walk towards him. Nervously they approached the soldiers, unsure what was happening. When close enough O'Neill grabbed them both by the arm, forcing them onto the floor.

Finn spoke, "We're British soldiers, SAS." He lifted the flap on his sleeve to show the union jack flag to confirm.

The man gestured as if he didn't understand the language, the woman began to speak, her voice cut off by the sound of bullets hitting the glass panels around them. Finn investigated the main room and noticed another man and woman entering via the airlock door. He swung his assault rifle around to the front of his body and joined O'Neill in a crouched position at the end of the corridor.

Finn recognised the blonde woman straight away, *Bergqvist*. As the man she had entered with fired the M249 machine gun, she began entering the code for the laboratory door. Currie and Heaney appeared from behind in support. Pinned down, with no cover and unable to enter the laboratories on either side he realised it was only a matter of time before the shooter began collecting bodies. He ordered his squad to take the scientists and retreat to the maintenance room. Bullets slammed into the area around the corridor, one hit O'Neill on the leg and the other soldiers quickly dragged him away.

Finn dived across the polished laboratory floor, sliding over to a solid based workstation in the middle of the room. Now closer to the shooter, and while crouching behind the unit, he held his assault rifle over the counter top and returned fire blindly.

One of Finn's stray bullets hit the magazine of the M249 and the firing stopped. The shooter pulled desperately at the breech, trying to free the jammed cartridge. Finn grabbed the opportunity, slid out from behind the workstation and took aim at the man's head. Bergqvist pushed open the laboratory door and dragged the shooter inside with her as Finn's bullet ripped a chunk of flesh from the man's ear. The shooter yelled as he dropped the M249 and blood splattered across the laboratory door.

Finn straightened up, advanced, and continued to shoot at the man making tiny marks on the bullet proof glass. He stopped shooting and stared at the big man on the other side of the glass who was laughing at him. Movement in the far corner of the lab momentarily distracted him. As he looked over the man's shoulder, he noticed Bergqvist entering a code into a large medical grade safe. Finn returned his attention to the man. His eyes narrowed as he read the man's name badge, *Wallenberg*.

Finn tried the laboratory door, finding it locked. He read the code on the keypad then pressed his comms button, "Charlie Five, I need door seven zero seven unlocking immediately, Alpha One out."

The IT guy in the server room heard his call sign and quickly began typing into a computer then responded, "Alpha one, opening now, Charlie Five out."

The lights on the keypad turned green and the lock made a clunk. Finn pushed the door open as Wallenberg approached with a hunting knife. Finn, seeing the danger, pulled his own knife as he entered. Once inside he heard the door lock again.

The two soldiers squared off, performing circular motions, left then right, maintaining the same distance apart. Finn noticed the other members of his squad appearing on the other side of the laboratory glass.

Wallenberg grinned and growled, "Come on then, let's see what you're made of tough guy."

Finn had a Deja Vu moment as the vision of Marcus* flashed through his mind...same size, hunting knife and bravado.

* see Finn's Quest.

Chapter 26
No Beginning, End

With all the airlocks now controlled by the IT guy in the server room, it was easy to trap most of the Existence members in their relative sectors.

In the main concourse Corporal Gray and his squad began gathering up the small number of civilians stationed there when the assault started. Most were confused, wandering around or hiding from the soldiers but a small number ganged together to protest. A young woman approached Hind and began shouting in a foreign language. He brushed her away, raised his gun to the air and shot a burst of bullets towards the tunnel ceiling. Splinters of rock dropped down and the group quickly dispersed.

Gray made a report, "All teams, we need support in the concourse, the locals are getting restless, also sections one to three are currently locked but unchecked. Delta One out."

Mac heard the call and signalled to the SAS soldiers with him to return to the concourse and support Gray and his squad.

Jones complained to Rowntree as they made their way there, "Great, we've been given the job of looking after a load of hippies?"

"Fifty percent are female and quite a lot of those are Swedish," Rowntree quipped.

"I suppose we'll cope."

As the SAS soldiers approached Gray shouted to Docherty, "Go and check that the tunnels leading to sections one to three are clear."

Docherty spotted a golf cart near the main airlock door, jumped in, and shouted for Hind and Herd to join him. Gray watched as they set off towards tunnel one.

Rowntree took another golf cart and headed off to tunnel six to collect the injured Borthwick, the IT guy looking after him and Ford's body.

The other soldiers began gathering up the civilians and the tied-up guards, moving everyone to one secure area. They guarded the prisoners, waiting to hear if the mission had been successful.

Mac and Petrikov entered the research sector airlock door finding Finn inside the laboratory room on their left. Standing outside the door Finn's squad watched, powerless to help their leader.

Mac shouted to O'Neill, "Why are you not going in there to help?"

O'Neill pointed towards Bergqvist inside the laboratory, "She has the weapon, if we go inside everyone will die. Our orders were to contain it."

Mac looked and noticed her standing next to the open safe door with a small silver case in her hand.

Finn and Wallenberg continued their dance both holding seven-inch hunting knives in a hammer grip. Finn assumed his assailant was as highly trained in knife combat as himself. Assuming anything less could prove damaging to his health. He constantly observed the Swede's hands and eyes, watching for the small tell-tale signs that would announce an imminent attack.

As Wallenberg lunged forward Finn kicked out. The Swede dodged the boot and Finn took the opportunity to advance, slicing his knife across the front of Wallenberg's body. A cut opened on the Swede's chest, causing him to look down as blood appeared on his jacket. With renewed determination he rushed towards Finn. The SAS soldier batted away the blade with his left arm and aimed his own blade at the Swede's left side.

Wallenberg predicted it and dodged to his right, then taunted, "Is that all you've got."

Finn grinned. The two men started a new dance, moving left to right waiting for round two to start. Finn kept his back towards the glass away from Bergqvist, who, from the rear of the lab was urging her lover on, "Go on kill him...Kill him!"

Finn quipped, "I'm trying!"

Wallenberg lunged forward with the knife in his right hand while trying to grab Finn's jacket with his free left. With an extra weight advantage Finn knew that it would be curtains if the Swede managed to get him on the floor. In defence, he stepped backwards then landed a blow with his left fist into the Swede's face. While rocked by the blow, Finn swung the knife in his right and sliced across Wallenberg's upper left arm.

A deep cut, down to the bone, appeared between the sliced material of the Swede's jacket.

With blood now oozing from the cuts on his chest, ear and arm Wallenberg's energy levels began to drop.

Finn noticed the balance of power swinging his way and advanced, going for the kill. He grabbed the Swede's blade hand with his left, pulled him closer then raised a knee into the groin.

Wallenberg began to double in pain. Finn sliced at the Swede's neck, as he drew the blade away a slice of flesh shot off with a trail of blood. Now living the final moments of his life Wallenberg dropped to his knees and looked up with pleading eyes. Finn ignored the look, moved behind the prone figure, pulled the head backwards and slit the Swede's throat.

Bergqvist screamed as Wallenberg fell forward, landing in a pool of blood.

Finn turned his attention towards the woman, her lovers' blood still dripping from his blade, "Give me that case and I'll let you live."

Bergqvist snapped open the case and showed Finn the contents, six test tubes. She noted the surprise on Finn's face and declared, "You're too late…the mission has already started."

"What have you done?" Finn growled.

"Even if you kill me, my legacy will live on, the message will still be delivered, in years to come people will remember what I tried to achieve here."

"Spare me the bullshit just tell me where the missing test tube is?"

She dropped her guard when she started laughing, allowing Finn the opportunity to advance towards her. He grabbed for the case. At the last moment Bergqvist swung herself away from him, and dropped the case.

The pair froze as the open case landed face down on the tiled floor. One single test tube rolled away and came to rest next to the safe. Realising the tube was intact Finn cursed and made another advance. Bergqvist ran around to the glass side of the laboratory.

She took up a kung foo stance in front of him and Finn quipped, "Who are you now, Bruce Lee's sister?"

As he spoke, she stepped forward and powered a fist into the centre of Finn's chest. The force of the punch knocked him backwards onto the floor. Finn looked up to see both Mac and Petrikov smiling at him through the glass window. He climbed to his feet and took up his own karate stance in front of her. Now with a renewed respect for her ability.

She advanced again, landing two rapid blows on Finn's face before swinging around, raising her leg as she moved and landing a heel into his ribs. The kick forced the air from his lungs and knocked him down again.

As he got up, she took up the stance again and motioned with her right hand for him to advance.

Finn accepted the invitation and rushed forward. He ducked under her defensive blow and hit her under the chin with his fist knocking her backwards. She landed on her back and immediately sprang up onto her feet resuming the kung foo stance.

Finn shook his head at her, "I'm impressed, you're definitely my type of woman. Maybe you should've accepted my offer when we last met."

She smiled and said, "You'll never know because we'll both be dead."

She ran over to the safe and picked up the test tube. Grabbed it with both hands she motioned to shatter the fragile glass. The thing that passed through her mind immediately after those suicidal thoughts was the blade of Finns thrown hunting knife. As she fell forward Finn dived across the room, slid under her body and cushioned her fall. He immediately flipped the dead body onto it's back and prised the test tube from the lifeless fingers.

Petrikov, Mac and the squad outside all sighed a breath of relief.

Finn gently turned over the small case and replaced the test tube. He looked around the room and found a medical grade incinerator unit in the corner.

He heard Mac on the comms system, "Charlie Five open door seven zero seven. Charlie One out." He reached the incinerator as the door lock engaged. Pulling open the incinerator he placed the case inside and locked the glass door.

Mac shouted, "Stop!"

Finn slammed his palm down on the Fire button and the inside chamber of the incinerator filled with flame vaporising all the biological material in a second.

He turned to Mac, "Sorry buddy no one nation deserves to own that stuff. Just forget about it, you need to focus your attention on a more pressing issue."

"What's that?" Mac asked.

"There's one test tube out in the open."

"How?"

From behind, Petrikov announced, "That bloody longhaired Swede!"

⁂

Mac made the call and within thirty minutes members of the Swedish army began arriving at the mine. The IT guy in the server room released the large outer doors and all the tunnel airlocks. Once inside, the Swedes began securing the facility marking the end of the work for the SAS soldiers. They grouped together and walked outside into the cold morning air carrying two body bags containing their fallen comrades, Ford, and Nolan. They waited in the car park outside the mine for new orders.

Chapter 27
Spirit of Sweden, Baltic Sea

The car ferry left on time. Lars found his cabin, a small room with two bunk beds and a small window. He pulled the top bunk down from the wall and stored his bag on it. He opened the door into the small toilet come shower cubicle, checking that it was empty.

He sat on the lower bunk and checked his mobile knowing that the signal would soon disappear once the ferry had left the port. *No messages.*

A feeling of disappointment engulfed him, surprised that she had not taken the time to reply to his previous messages. He shrugged it off. *She must be busy.*

With moments to spare before losing the network he typed a new message. *'On my way to Saint Petersburg. All clear so far. Ferry on time. I will text again once I am past Russian customs. I miss you. I think I am in love.'*

Petrikov picked up the mobile call, "Yes."

"Major it's Khristina. I've intercepted a message from the Swedish mobile. The user is currently travelling by car ferry, the *'Spirit of Sweden'*, heading to Saint Petersburg. The ship sailed thirty minutes ago and is due to arrive in Russia in thirty-eight hours."

"Is the phone still transmitting?"

"No sir, it's now outside of the mobile network. It'll be silent for the duration unless the user buys air time on the ship."

"Continue to monitor it anyway."

"Yes sir."

Petrikov hung up the phone and looked at both Finn and Mac, "My people have traced Lars. We must assume that he has the weapon. His last transmission was from a car ferry on its way to Russia. It will arrive in Saint Petersburg in thirty-eight hours."

"It's on a car ferry?" Mac asked.

Finn said, "Which one of you two gentlemen can get hold of a helicopter straightaway?"

"What are you thinking?" Mac asked.

"It's simple, we need to get on that ship and neutralise the weapon and the operator, this Lars guy. The alternative is we fail and the device goes off and it's only the ferry occupants that are affected."

Petrikov said, "It sounds like a suicide mission. If we corner him, he may set it off anyway."

"Well, it's either that or sitting on our arses and doing nothing. I don't like doing nothing. Have you both got something else planned?" Finn said sarcastically.

Petrikov took out his mobile and called Roslakova, "Lieutenant, I need a helicopter. Which air base is closest to my current location?"

The line went quiet for several minutes before she replied, "Major the nearest is Olenya Air Base. It's a Navy reconnaissance and long-range bomber base on the Kola peninsula, south of Murmansk."

"Get to the point Lieutenant! Just give me the number of who's in charge, I don't need a full in-depth analysis of the place."

Petrikov wrote down the details, hung up then called Olenya and demanded to speak to the base commander. After a short call a Kamov Ka-60 helicopter was airborne on the three-hundred-and-ten-mile journey to Kiruna airport.

The two-hour flight allowed time for the assault teams to return to their vehicles and drive to Kiruna, under escort from the Swedish military.

At a secure section of the airport Finn, Mac and Petrikov stripped down to basic fatigues in a changing room, normally used by ground crew. They grabbed some coats and hats from the lockers to supplement their appearance. Standing together they appeared like a group of hunters on holiday, each with a pistol as a weapon.

Corporal Gray approached Finn and asked, "How many of us are going with you sir?"

"None!" Finn barked. "Once we're in the air take the vehicles and get to the safehouse. Wait there. A Chinook is coming to collect the squad, including the injured and bodies. I'll see you at Hereford."

Corporal Gray saluted then returned to the men waiting around the vehicles.

Finn looked at his watch, *07:28,* then turned his attention to Petrikov and Mac, "If he's already on the ferry then at least he's contained. Also, we don't want to start a panic with the passengers so we need to do this covertly. How far is it from here to the ferry?"

Petrikov responded, "About seven hundred miles. We'll need to refuel the helicopter in Finland. Olenya is making the arrangements. Once the refuelling is complete, we'll intercept the ferry while it's in the middle of the Baltic Sea. If there's an accident and the biological material escapes, the fallout will only affect the area around the ship. I've put the Russian helicopter base on Gogland Island on standby. If we fail then they've got orders to sink the ship. We're looking at another six hours to reach the ship after we take off from here."

"That means we'll arrive at the ferry around fourteen hundred hours," Mac confirmed, after consulting his watch.

In the distance the sound of a helicopter approaching broke their concentration. The sound grew louder as a large green helicopter with a red star on the side appeared out of the clouds above them. As it began hovering over the airport O'Neill threw a red flare onto the ground to mark the landing zone. The pilot circled a couple of times to confirm that it was safe then touched down. The co-pilot opened the cargo door and Finn, Petrikov and Mac climbed in.

Corporal Jones and Docherty helped with the gear then continued standing with the rest of the attack force. They watched as the Russian helicopter took off and disappeared into the clouds. As ordered, they loaded the two body bags

249

into the Landcruiser, climbed into the vehicles, left the airport and returned to the safehouse.

The Ka-60 flew in a straight line, heading towards the refuelling point in Finland. It climbed to twelve thousand feet whilst over Swedish territory and the Gulf of Bothnia. As the helicopter approached Finnish air space the pilot descended to low level, adopting nap-of-the-earth tactics to avoid radar detection. The pilot displayed excellent flying skills as he flew at tree level and between hills and mountains.

With the fuel warning lights flashing the helicopter landed at a secluded airport in the south of Finland. A Russian Mi-10 heavy lift helicopter ferried a fuel tanker over the border from Russia to the landing strip along with a set of engineers. Once refuelled the Ka-60 continued onwards towards the ferry. The Mi-10 returned over the border to Russia. By the time the Finnish Air Force had noticed the intrusion both helicopters were long gone.

Petrikov spoke to the Ka-60 pilot in Russian then relayed the information to the others, "It's another hour and a half until we intercept the ferry. The helicopter will continue to the Russian air base at Gogland Island. It won't have enough fuel to take us back."

Finn said dryly, "We'll not need it anyway. If we fail, we'll be dead and if we succeed, we'll be going to the bar to celebrate."

Petrikov patted him on the shoulder, "Too true my friend."

❖ ❖ ❖ ❖

Mac pointed out of the window, "There she is."

The others looked, spotting the large white car ferry fighting the waves of the Baltic Sea.

"What do we know about the ship?" Finn asked.

"My guys have sent over a deck plan and a description, hang on a second." Mac pulled out the iBOW and opened the email from the intelligence officer at Gällivare. He began reading out the report for the others, shouting above the noise of the helicopter blades, "Six hundred and ninety-five feet long, forty-eight thousand tonnes and ten decks. Decks ten to six are passenger decks, the lower ones are for vehicles and employees. There can be anything up to two thousand eight hundred passengers and crew. From the passenger manifest they've managed to identify Lars as the passenger in cabin eight one two four. It will be no surprise that you'll find it on deck eight. He's driving a Red Range Rover, the one you discovered at Bergqvist's house, it's parked somewhere on car deck four. You'll just have to get down there and look for it."

Finn looked over the deck plans then asked Petrikov, "Can you get the pilot to drop us off at the rear of the ship, on deck nine."

Mac passed the iBOW displaying the deck plan image to Petrikov who showed it to the Russian pilot. After a short conversation he returned it and said, "Agreed."

❖ ❖ ❖ ❖

The three men quickly checked their gear. Finn secured the one-point six-inch rope, required for them to fast rope onto the ferry deck to a hook.

The ferry captain observed the low flying helicopter approaching on the horizon. Assuming it was just another military helicopter patrolling the area, he ignored it.

The pilot guided the helicopter along the side of the ferry. As it passed the stern of the ship, he swung the helicopter around one hundred and eighty degrees and began flying directly behind it, undetected from the ferry bridge. The weather helped to board the ship undetected because the Captain closed the outer decks to passengers.

The three men readied themselves as the co-pilot opened the cargo door. The wind and sea spray soaked Petrikov and he cursed. Mac and Finn grinned at him.

The pilot pulled the helicopter up to a higher altitude and Finn threw the rope out of the cargo door. The co-pilot guided the pilot as he moved the helicopter forward until the end of the rope came to rest on the rear of deck nine. The co-pilot shouted in Russian and patted Finn on the shoulder. Without hesitation he gripped the rope and jumped. The other two followed at the three-meter intervals. Finn landed on the wet deck and took up a defensive position with his pistol drawn as Mac and Petrikov joined him. Finn put away the pistol once he was sure they had managed to board undetected. Petrikov waved to the helicopter co-pilot who began pulling in the heavy rope while the helicopter climbed and moved away.

From the window on the bridge wing, the second officer watched the helicopter and said to the Captain, "What do you think they were looking for?"

"Don't worry about the Russian helicopters. The helicopter base at Gogland does regular patrols around here, monitoring the shipping. It's an early warning station for their Northern fleet, they have no interest in a car ferry. Keep your attention on our ship."

As agreed, Mac headed to the bridge, Finn headed to the car deck and Petrikov headed towards the passenger decks. With their basic fatigues and coats they quickly blended in with the tourists and truckers enjoying the recreation areas. All three had stashed their silenced pistols in the back of their cargo pants.

Mac used the outer walkway of deck nine, climbed a set of stairs to deck ten, ran along the top of the ship past the helipad towards the front of the ship. As he approached the bridge, he took a stairway down to deck nine. He jumped over a chain with a *'No Public Access'* sign and continued to the bridge door. He swung the door open and walked calmly into the bridge with his pistol drawn, catching the bridge crew off guard.

Picking out the Captain he said, "Relax, I'm here with two colleagues to secure a dangerous passenger. As soon as we've collected him, we'll be out of your hair. Just continue as normal."

"Why haven't I been told about this? You're English...Were you on that Russian helicopter? What is going on? It's illegal to board a ship in international waters, I'll…"

Mac approached the Captain, "If you don't shut the hell up complaining, I'll shoot you and your friend here will gain a promotion. Do you understand?"

The Captain looked at the pistol, looked blankly at Mac then looked around at the petrified bridge crew and shouted, "Watch your panels."

The staff continued with their work and the Captain turned to Mac, "There'd better be a good explanation for this."

Mac said dryly, "Believe me when I say it's a matter of life and death."

❖ ❖ ❖ ❖

Finn moved through the rear deck access doors and walked along the corridor between the passenger cabins. He arrived at the rear staircase and gradually descended until he reached car deck four. He pressed the large button next to the bulkhead door. Nothing happened. He read the large sign on the door. *'No access to car deck during sailing'*

He cursed then returned up the stairs to deck six and headed forward through the passenger recreation area. He walked through the buffet and into the main bar. A drunk

Russian was singing a song, badly, on Karaoke. A group of men standing at the bar cheered, urging the man to continue making a fool of himself.

Finn laughed to himself as he continued onwards to the central staircase. He ventured down to vehicle deck four access door and got the same result. He looked up and noticed a security camera guarding the door. He moved against the wall and hid under the staircase. He was in the process of considering his options when a maintenance engineer in bright orange overalls came down the staircase. He watched as the engineer put a key card into a lock on the wall then pressed the access button. The hydraulic mechanism activated and the heavy bulkhead door slid open. The engineer disappeared inside. Finn moved quickly to follow him and reached the vehicle deck in time to see the door shut behind him.

He crouched down next to a grey BMW and watched as the engineer continued walking away from him towards the front of the ship. At the rear corner of the BMW, he moved ninety degrees and progressed between the BMW back bumper and the front of a Ford van. He straightened up and could now see three rows of vehicles stretched out in front of him, a mixture of cars, large and small vans, mobile homes, and caravans. He stayed in the middle row and moved towards the rear of the ship.

As he approached the rear loading ramp, he spotted a set of dirty overalls hanging over a railing. The original bright orange colour now covered in oily patches. He quickly pulled the overalls on over his clothes. The clothes reduced his chances of detection while searching for the Range Rover.

At the rear loading ramp, he walked around to the second set of three rows of vehicles leading up the other side of the ship. On the far side, near the middle he spotted the large red SUV.

He worked his way to the vehicle and looked through the windows. The rear seats down and a large aluminium flight case took up the space in the boot. He crouched down at the rear hatch and took out the code scanner that the intelligence officer had given him. After a few minutes the display on the scanner turned green and the locks on the Rover popped open.

He opened the rear hatch and opened the latches on the aluminium flight case, slowly lifting the lid before discarding it onto the deck at the side of the vehicle. Inside he found the gas bottles and a digital panel with a sequence of rotating red LED's that told him the device was active.

Finn searched the interior of the vehicle for the trigger mechanism then realised that the Swede must have taken it to his cabin.

Petrikov moved in through the rear doors on deck nine, watching Finn walking in the port side corridor ahead of him. He cut between the passenger cabins to the starboard side corridor and continued forward. At the rear staircase he moved down to deck eight then looked for a deck plan, finding it on the wall next to a lift. He quickly searched for cabin eight one two four, it was located at the front on the port side. Realising he was on the wrong side of the ship he headed down the corridor past the central staircase and onwards to the front. At the forward staircase he took the opportunity to cut across to the port side.

As he approached Lars's cabin, he slowed down and removed the pistol from his belt, holding it low to his side to ensure that it remained undetected by the corridor security cameras.

He banged on the cabin door. No answer. He banged again. No answer. *Shit!*

Stashing the pistol, he decided to move down to deck six and the passenger recreation area. Aware of the fact that Lars may spot him he pulled his hat lower, partially covering his face. He entered the bar area and finding the Karaoke in full swing moved to the shadows near the windows. Looking around he visually scanned the tables and chairs containing partying passengers, groups of tourists and truckers enjoying the entertainment and drinks. Having confirmed to himself that the Swede was not among the passengers he moved out of the bar and into the buffet restaurant. Walking between the rows of tables he checked the table occupants while trying to not make it obvious. *Nothing.*

He continued down the corridor and into a large lounge area where the people who had not paid for cabins had taken up station on the bench seats. Mainly groups of young men and women on vacation. All around the deck impromptu parties had been set up with music, food, and alcohol shared and enjoyed. In the far corner he noticed a group of young women. To their side a blonde-haired man with his back turned to him, was talking to a woman. The size, shape and ponytail told him that he had found his target.

To get closer he dodged the obstacles on the floor, cases, bags, boxes of beer and rubbish. He stepped on a young couple sleeping on the floor and was about to apologise only to realise they were out cold, stone drunk. He moved between a row of bench seats, now within twenty feet of the man, taking his eyes off the floor for a split second, only to fall over a suitcase. He cursed as he landed on a group of young men playing cards on the floor. As he began to get back to his feet, he noticed the Swede had turned around to see what the commotion was.

The Swede laughed at the large man on the floor and made a clever comment to the woman, ridiculing the unfortunate tourist. As Petrikov pulled himself fully up onto his feet the two men's eyes met.

Lars recognised the tourist but it was a few seconds later before his brain told him why. He shoved the young woman towards the Russian and began running. He headed towards the outer deck door, finding it blocked with a safety chain. After pulling at the flimsy chain to remove it he managed to push the door open.

Petrikov, now ten feet behind, followed him through the same door onto the outer deck which was wet from sea spray. The rolling of the ship also made moving quickly very difficult. He slipped, lost his footing, and crashed into the guard rail. For a moment he thought he was going to go over the side of the ship, grabbing the guard rail at the last second to stop his progress. Once safely back on his feet he looked along the deck only to see the Swede getting further away. In an instant he was running.

Lars quickly opened a door into the interior of the ship, Petrikov followed into a corridor containing cabins. Half way down he noticed Lars using his key card in the door lock. He ran towards him and the Swede opened the cabin door and disappeared inside.

Petrikov threw his full weight against the flimsy cabin door and it burst open. As he entered the room Lars grabbed at the bag on the top bunk and pulled out the weapon trigger mechanism. Sensing the danger, he advanced into the small room and threw a heavy punch into the Swede's face.

The blow forced Lars to fall backwards against the porthole window. The two men paused for a moment as the trigger dropped onto the floor and spun away under the bottom bunk.

Petrikov grabbed the Swede by the throat with both of his hands. Lars retaliated by punching him in the ribs with a series of powerful blows that knocked the air from the Russian's lungs. Petrikov released the grip on the Swede's throat as he gasped for air. Lars took the opportunity to land a fist into his face, breaking the nose that had only just begun to heal. Blood poured down the Russian's face and a large grin appeared on Lars's face.

Enraged, Petrikov landed a series of blows to the Swede's face, repaying the compliment. Lars's nose and lip burst open. In response the Swede raised a knee into the Russian's groin.

Gripping pain tore through Petrikov's body as he collapsed in a heap holding onto his damaged tackle. As he bent forward Lars landed another powerful blow into his face and he toppled over onto his back. While he was down Lars took the opportunity, dived on top of him and reached under the bed.

In an instance Lars returned to his feet with the trigger in his hand. He smiled at Petrikov, noting the worried look on the prone Russian's face. He began typing the activation code into the handset. The digital display turned green, confirming the dispersion device in the Rover was also ready.

"You seem to have nine lives or a guardian angel my Russian friend. I was sure I'd killed you in Helsinki."

"We'll both be dead if you press that trigger," Petrikov advised.

"We can go to hell together but the message will still be delivered to the leaders of the world."

Petrikov pleaded, "Put it down, the mission is over, there will never be a message. The Russian Navy is getting ready to sink the ferry, an unfortunate shipping incident that will be swept under the carpet."

The expression on Lars's face changed to one of confusion, "What...What are you saying…"

Petrikov got up from the floor and held hands out in a submissive stance, "Look, we can work something out, I promise you that you'll go free, no charges, just hand it over."

"What...I don't understand..."

"Your mission is over, the revolution has failed, we have the biological substance."

"Revolution...What are you saying?"

"It's over, the game is up, Början has been destroyed, put the trigger down."

"Destroyed...But...What about?"

"Bergqvist? She's dead."

As the words came out of his mouth Petrikov wished he could pull them back. A look of horror appeared on the Swede's face. He cried out in pain...then pressed the trigger.

❖ ❖ ❖ ❖

Finn became exasperated. He had wasted enough time considering what to do to disarm the device. In desperation he considered pulling all the wires out of the display. As he got hold of the wires the red LEDs on the device display began spinning faster. A loud tone sounded and the display turned green. The mechanism made a loud hissing noise and gas began escaping from the bottles.

Finn stepped away from the rear of the Range Rover as a mist surrounded him. He held his breath as the mist grew larger and began filling the whole vehicle deck. He instinctively moved away from the device, feeling his way through the mist. The lack of oxygen made him feel lightheaded and his face began to turn blue. Remembering that the scientists had said that skin would also absorb the biological substance he gave in and filled his lungs with air and mist.

❖ ❖ ❖ ❖

Lars continued to scream as he held the trigger button down. Petrikov pulled out his pistol and shot the Swede in the leg. Lars collapsed down onto one knee and the Russian kicked him in the face, knocking him out cold.

The trigger rolled from Lars' hand, onto the floor, Petrikov reached down, picked it up and looked at the green flashing display. He waited, expecting life to be torn from his body, like the unfortunate inhabitants of Yacheyka. Waiting for the biological weapon to begin breaking down the cells in his body, spreading and advancing until it had consumed everything. Leaving his corpse as a blackened shell, a receptacle to hold the deadly spores of the pathogen until a new host came along.

Lars distracted him from his morbid thoughts, moaning as he slowly regained consciousness. Petrikov kicked him in the head and he passed out again. He returned to his thoughts and waited.

A smoky mist began filling the cabin from the ventilation duct on the ceiling. He picked up a pillow to block the vent only to see the mist coming in from a crack under the door. The cabin filled with mist and he considered the final moments of his life. After a short period of time, he became confused, the mist had surrounded him but he was still breathing. *Why am I still alive?*

He waited for a few more moments, surely death will happen soon. *Nothing. Eh...*

Bored with waiting for death to claim him, Petrikov decided to complete his mission. He grabbed Lars by the feet and dragged the unconscious body out of the cabin into the corridor. He continued along the corridor, heading towards the outer deck access doorway. Passengers flooded out of the cabins in panic. He shouted in Russian for the people to get out of his way.

On the outer deck Petrikov lifted the Swede's legs, taking a foot in each hand. A grin appeared on his face as he parted the legs into a 'V' shape.

Lars began to wake, groaning in pain, "Why are we still alive?"

Petrikov stamped down hard with the heel of his boot into the Swede's groin. Lars passed out with the searing pain, "You won't be needing them where you're going shithead."

Pleased with himself he grabbed Lars's limp body under the arms, heaved it up, and propped it against the guardrail. He stepped backwards then threw a final powerful punch into the Swede's face.

The force of the blow made Lars body pivot on the top of the guardrail and fall over the side. Petrikov watched as it disappeared under the waves.

Finn continued standing in the middle of the cloud of mist waiting to die. Disappointed by the lack of progress he walked slowly towards the vehicle deck access door. *Nothing.*

He walked up the staircase and up to deck eight. *Still nothing.*

A call came over the ships speaker system, *"Ladies and gentlemen this is the Captain. Please do not be alarmed. We have a fault on the ship sprinkler system. This will be rectified soon. Please return to your cabins."*

Finn headed towards Lars's cabin, finding signs of a struggle and the trigger mechanism on the floor still flashing.

A passenger spoke in a foreign language and Finn replied, "Sorry, do you speak English?"

"Are you looking for the Russian?"

"Yes."

"His friend was struggling to breath. He took him outside for fresh air."

Finn found Petrikov on the outer deck propped up against the guardrail. The two men stared at each other with puzzled faces.

Finn broke the silence, "Where's the Swede?"

"Taking a swim."

"The device went off but nothing happened."

Petrikov shrugged his shoulders, "You sound disappointed?"

Finn noted the pain etched into the Russians face, "Are 'they' still causing you problems?"

"My dear friend it'll be a long time before I ride a horse again."

The two men laughed together. Finn helped Petrikov to the bridge via the bar. After a couple of quick vodkas, they made their way up to the bridge to meet up with Mac.

On the top deck of the ferry a Swedish Air Force helicopter landed on the helipad. Mac shook hands with the Captain, then the three men made their way to the helipad. After a brief discussion with the pilot, they began the long journey back to Stockholm.

In the helicopter Mac announced, "While I was on the bridge, I got a call from the team at the mine."

The other two stared back with blank faces, too tired to care. Petrikov fell into a deep sleep. The throbbing of the rotor blades mixed with the Russian's snoring reminded Finn of the fishing boat. He closed his eyes and joined the Russian. Mac gave up and looked out of the window.

The Swedish soldiers cleared the tunnels and gathered the occupants of the mine outside. In each empty tunnel the

Army engineers planted charges, ready for the destruction of the facility.

Molantra sat on a pile of stones and watched as people spilled out of the mine entrance into the night air, dazed, confused and lucky to be alive.

The chemist took up a spot next to him. Together they began laughing, giggling like school children.

From his inside jacket pocket Molantra slowly removed a test tube containing a blue liquid.

Epilogue

Mac and Finn found Petrikov standing near the Ka-60 helicopter that had arrived to collect the Russian soldier.

The MI6 man shook his hand, "Thanks for all your help Vanya, no doubt our paths will cross again."

Petrikov accepted the gesture and turned to Finn who added, "It's definitely been an adventure Major, stay safe."

"Yes, you're right my SAS friend, it's been an adventure all right. You've completed your mission and I've also achieved what I set out to do."

"You mean making sure that the weapon could not fall into the wrong hands?"

Petrikov laughed, patted the breast pocket of his uniform, and spoke to himself in Russian.

"What's that you're saying?" Finn asked.

"I was just saying a prayer for my grandfather."

"Your grandfather? What made you think of him?"

"I always think of him, Major General Vladimir Petrikov."

"He's in the army?

"He was. He's dead now. He died in nineteen sixty-four."

"I'm sorry to hear that," Finn said sympathetically. "To win the Russian Gold Star medal I can only assume he was an exceptional soldier, and very brave, you'll be proud."

"Very proud. He was the inspiration for my life, the reason I joined the military."

Petrikov leaned forward, "I'll tell you a story my good friend. There was a Russian soldier who won the Gold Star for bravery in the second world war. He survived many battles and progressed through the ranks. His final assignment before retirement was as head of security at a research facility."

Finn was intrigued, "A research facility?"

"One day there was an accident and he was killed in a horrible way, when he deserved to die in battle."

A word came into Finn's head, "Yacheyka!"

Petrikov nodded, put his fingers into the breast pocket and pulled out a medal, a gold star on a red ribbon.

The penny dropped as Finn said, "The bank!"

THE END

Abbreviations and Notes

SAS - Special Air Service (British army, founded 1941)

MI6 – The UK foreign intelligence service with the task of covert overseas collection and analysis of human intelligence in support of the UK's national security. Also known as the Secret Intelligence Service (SIS).

Bootneck – A nickname for a Royal Marine. It refers to the leather strap that Marines used to cut from their boots and wrap around their necks to stop attackers slitting their throats.

POTUS - President of the United States

MP - Military Police

SIG Sauer P320 - Semi-automatic Pistol.

Heckler & Koch HK416 - Assault Rifle.

Heckler & Koch MP5 - Machine Pistol.

GSh-18PT – 9 mm Semi-automatic Pistol.

M249 - Belt-fed Light Machine Gun.

iBOW - military grade communication device used for various tasks…making calls, taking photos, messaging, GPS route planning and information storage. Data transfer uses encryption software. (Fictitious – the author created the name iBOW to avoid confusion with other devices.)

Printed in Great Britain
by Amazon